Her Cowboy Baby Daddy

Her Cowboy Baby Daddy

A Return to Keller Ranch Romance

Jeannie Watt

TULE
PUBLISHING

Chapter One

"I CAN'T DO it." Spence Keller shifted his phone as he slowed his '98 Chevy Silverado pickup and turned onto the road leading to the family ranch. The wheels bounced over the cattle guard with a familiar rattle as he drove under the old log archway.

"Are you sure?" Millie Carney, never one to take the first "no" seriously, proceeded to list all the reasons that Spence couldn't afford to pass up the welding contract Carney Construction was offering.

"Millie, I appreciate the offer," Spence said when she paused for breath, "and I may be available in the fall, but for now, I have a commitment." With his dad looking at a second back surgery, Spence was needed on the ranch, and that was where he was going to be.

He and his brother Reed would keep the home fires burning, and hopefully, keep their dad out of commission long enough for him to heal. Daniel Keller had a reputation for pushing the envelope, and it would probably take both Spence and Reed to keep him contained during the busy time on the ranch.

Millie's sigh was loud and long. "You're my best guy."

Spence smiled a little. "I bet you say that to all the welders." He turned his head as a flash of red in the undergrowth near the creek caught his eye. He automatically slowed down, and a second later, he caught another flash of red. "Thanks for the offer, Millie. I'll let you know when I'm done here. I've got to go."

"Stay in touch," Millie said rather than goodbye.

She barely got the last word out before Spence ended the call and pulled his truck to the side of the road. He rolled down the window and studied the area where he saw the color that didn't belong. It could be a scrap of trash blowing through the brush, or . . . a small dog wearing a red neoprene vest.

Huh.

Spence opened his door as the little dog sank into the tall grass, watching him from between the blades with wide brown eyes. Lost and afraid, it lowered its head uncertainly as he stepped to the ground.

"Hey, little one. You lost?"

The dog crouched lower.

Spence crossed the road, hoping that the pup didn't jet back into the underbrush. As he got closer, the dog hunched its shoulders, as if trying to make itself invisible. Spence gently scooped it up with one hand.

"Hey there. Where do you belong?"

The neoprene vest was nearly new, with the loop of

white plastic that had held the price tag still in place. It was odd that someone would spend the money for a pricey vest, but not bother with a name tag.

Spence held the dog against his shoulder and scanned the country around him. The Keller Ranch was bordered on the far side by the Hunt Ranch, nearly two miles away, and on the side where he now stood by the Lone Tree Ranch. Everything else was federal land. The little dog could have gotten lost from a campsite, or she could have crossed the Keller Ranch from the Hunt Ranch, or she had strayed from the Lone Tree Ranch. The Parker family, who owned the Lone Tree, were not the kind of people who put dogs in expensive neoprene vests. But they might know someone who did.

Spence carried the dog back to the truck and, after closing the door to make certain she didn't try to bolt at the last minute, he gently set the quivering terrier on the seat beside him. She inched closer and set her chin on his thigh, officially melting his heart.

"We'll find your folks," he promised her. He put the truck in gear and drove to the nearest wide spot, executed a three-point turn, then headed back in the direction from which he'd come. The Lone Tree Ranch turnoff from another mile up the county road. Spence made the turn, then drove east for another mile before pulling into the property.

Hank Parker had died almost two years ago, and his

daughter Hayley had taken over. From the looks of things, she'd poured a lot of energy into property maintenance. The buildings were old, but freshly painted, the driveway newly graveled. A large, neatly laid out garden was protected by a deer fence, and the flower beds bordering the front of the house were immaculate.

Hayley always had been an overachiever, noted for both her academic prowess and her shyness. Spence's friends had joked about her being so quiet that no one realized she was there while they were talking, thus allowing her to know a lot of deep, dark secrets. Spence didn't know if that had been true, but he did know from firsthand experience that quiet Hayley Parker had a backbone of steel.

The little dog jumped to her feet as soon as they'd passed the main ranch gate and now stood with her hind feet on the seat and her front paws on the passenger-side window ledge, her nose pressed to the glass. Maybe the Parkers did believe in dog clothes.

He stopped the truck and got out, leaving it idling. The little dog now had her nose pressed against the driver's window. If she wasn't home, then she was in a place she liked.

He started for the house, but a clattering noise in the barn on the opposite side of the driveway caused him to change direction.

"Hello?" he called as he approached the open bay doors.

"Vince?" A muffled feminine voice sounded from the

backside of the tractor. "You're late."

"Not Vince," Spence said.

A wrench clattered to the ground, followed by a muffled curse, then Hayley Parker walked around the back of the tractor, coming to a stop near the wide rear tire. It appeared to take her a second to recognize him, although Spence would have known her anywhere. Her auburn hair fell around her shoulders instead of being caught up in the low ponytails she'd favored when they'd gone to school together, and the glasses were gone, but other than that, she'd barely changed.

Had he?

He didn't think so, so maybe it was the shock of seeing one of the nomad Kellers in the vicinity that put that surprised look on her face.

"Spence. It's been a while."

He smiled and noticed that she didn't drop her gaze after speaking, like she used to. "It has. I'm home until fall, helping. Dad is having back surgery at the end of the month."

"So you stopped by to say hello?" she asked.

He felt color creep up his neck. That would have been the neighborly thing to do, considering how she'd done him a solid back in the day, but the truth was that he'd never thought to stop and say hello to his shy neighbor. Once their adventure had ended, Hayley had seemed fine never speaking to him again, putting their relationship back where it had been before she'd saved his ass. A nod in the hallways when they'd passed one another, but only if she couldn't pretend that she didn't see him.

Spence was still searching for a suitable reply when Hayley suddenly smiled. "It's good to see you, Spence."

He tipped his head to one side. She'd been teasing him? Hayley Parker wasn't the type who teased. Or at least he hadn't read her that way back when he'd been a thick-headed teen. He allowed himself a half smile as he met her challenge.

"What if I am here to say hello?"

She pretended to consider, then shook her head. "I don't see it happening."

He spread his hands. "Yet here I am."

She crossed her arms and shifted her weight, a faint smile still playing on her lips as she lifted her eyebrows. "*Did* you stop to say hello?"

"I stopped because I found a dog."

"Really?" She came out from where she'd stood half-shielded by the tractor tire, suddenly interested. "What kind of dog?"

"A small one. Scruffy hair. Wearing a red harness thing." As he spoke, he knew that he was probably going to have a dog on his hands for a while, because Hayley did not seem to own the animal.

"Do you have the dog with you?"

"I do." He motioned toward his truck with his head, and together they walked through the open bay door and across the driveway. "Indulging in a little tractor repair?" he asked as they crossed the gravel. He was surprised; not because she was a woman—no brother of Em Keller was going to make that mistake—but because she'd always been so deeply academic.

Perhaps the way she'd gotten you out of the shed should have clued you in to the fact that she had hidden skills.

Indeed, it would have, if he hadn't been so focused on making the big game.

"Maintained equipment lasts longer." She glanced up at him as if to ascertain whether he was aware of that life hack.

He was, but he wasn't familiar with this not-so-shy side of Hayley. Well, it had been over a decade since they'd last spoken, when she'd graduated high school the same year as his younger twin siblings, Cade and Em.

The dog came alive when Hayley leaned into the truck.

"What have you been up to, Greta?" she said to the wiggling terrier, before glancing up at Spence. "I know this dog."

"No kidding."

"I fostered her before she found her forever home."

"I found her beside the road, hiding in the bushes. Any idea who adopted her?"

"Someone on the Hunt Ranch."

So his least likely scenario—that the little dog had crossed Keller property from the Hunt Ranch—was the correct one. Huh. She didn't look like she had that many miles in her short legs, but he couldn't say he faulted her for leaving the Hunt Ranch. He had issues with the management there.

"Do you want me to deliver her home?" he asked.

"Why don't you leave her with me, and I'll contact the shelter, and we'll work it from that angle."

"You're sure?"

The dog climbed into her arms. "I am," she said, rubbing the dog's ears, before giving him a sideways look. "I'm glad you found her."

"Yeah." He pushed his hands into his rear pockets. Time to go, but he wasn't quite ready. The change in Hayley was intriguing. Gone was the girl who rarely met your gaze and in her place was a confident woman.

"Have you been home long?" he asked.

She gave him a curious look and once again he felt as if he'd put his foot in it. They were neighbors, with a narrow strip of federal land separating the two ranches, but he'd left home at eighteen, returning only for holidays and family emergencies, while Hayley had . . .

He didn't have a clue what she'd done.

"I don't spend much time here," he said. "Work keeps me on the move, so I'm not up on community news."

She gave a faint shrug. "After I finished college, I moved back home, and Dad and I ran the ranch together until he passed away."

"Did you get a degree in Ag?"

Her smile twisted in a self-deprecating way and again he was struck by the way she met his gaze instead of glancing down. "Nothing as useful as that. I majored in English Lit with a minor in education."

"But you're not teaching?" It was a Wednesday in early May. A workday.

"A lot of ranch work to be done," she said simply.

"You have help, right?"

"I do." She left it at that. Looking around, Spence had to assume she had competent help because the place was immaculate. New roofs on the buildings. Late spring flowers bordering the two-rail fence bordering the front yard. The only project he could see in progress was the half-finished corral near the barn. A pile of pipe lay in front of the completed section, rusty from the weather, making him wonder how long the construction hiatus had been going on.

But rusty pipe aside, Hayley Parker appeared to have a handle on life . . . as did he. It wasn't your normal existence, taking welding contracts all over the west, having no real home base, drifting here and there, but it suited him. And for the life of him, he didn't know why. He just liked being able to pick up and go whenever he wanted or needed to. He had a feeling it was a latent gene from his wild man father; however, his mom's dad had also been born under the proverbial wandering star. Maybe he had no choice. He was wired to roam.

"It was good seeing you, Spence." Hayley hugged the

dog to her shoulder as she stepped away from the truck, clearing the way for him to get into the driver's seat. Spence took the hint.

He got into the truck, then leaned an arm on the window frame. "I don't think I properly thanked you for saving me that night in high school." He wanted her to know that he still appreciated all she'd done for him.

"You didn't." She shrugged. "Unless you call steering clear of me a gesture of thanks."

Spence's eyebrows drew together at the candid reply. "I thought you wanted it that way." She'd certainly been no friendlier after their adventure. If anything, she appeared to avoid looking at him. He'd honestly assumed that she wanted little to do with him after being shocked when she'd walked by him the following day in the hall without more than a quick glance.

She considered, then said, "I can't fault you for that. I wasn't good at putting myself out there back then." She put a slight emphasis on the last words. "I needed . . . I don't know . . . help?"

"Which I didn't give," he admitted. "Sorry about that, because I owed you." The entire varsity basketball team owed her. He'd been top scorer that night, and Lucas Barstow, whom he was certain had locked him in the equipment shed, fouled out early on. Lucas had planned to be the big hero, and he wasn't, thanks to Hayley.

"You did owe me," she agreed with no hint of blame.

"The important thing is that I got you to the game."

"I was having some doubts about whether we'd make it when the cop pulled us over."

Hayley made a small dismissive hand gesture, as if talking a cop out of a ticket was all in a day's work. She'd done a helluva job of it too. Spence, who'd thought life as he knew it was over when the reds and blues had shown in the rear window, had been beyond stunned when Hayley managed to get them back on the road in a matter of minutes.

"Never doubt me." She met his eyes and smiled while idly stroking the dog's ears. Now he felt like dropping his gaze.

"You've changed," he said.

As soon as he said the words, he knew he was wrong. She hadn't changed. She'd tapped into whatever had given her the moxie to sweet-talk the cop that night. And to break the hasp on the equipment shed to let him out.

"We all grow up, Spence."

He wasn't certain how to take the statement and was debating a reply when a small Jeep came into sight on the far side of the big pasture where Hayley's Angus grazed.

"Vince, my foreman. I need to get this little girl situated and get back to work. Thanks again, Spence. I'm glad you found her."

"No problem." The words came out gruffly. Nothing like being reminded that you were a self-centered teen to brighten the day.

He lifted a hand, then wheeled the truck around onto the driveway. He glanced in the rearview mirror, saw that Hayley was watching him go, and let his gaze linger longer than he should have. A split second later he jerked the steering wheel hard to the left to avoid hitting the gatepost.

Nice going, Keller.

He resisted the temptation to check the mirror again and continued down the driveway. One showy maneuver per visit was his limit.

HAYLEY SNUGGLED THE dog under her chin as she watched Spence Keller abruptly change the trajectory of his truck. Thank goodness her gatepost was still standing.

She turned her back to the dust cloud settling on the driveway and started toward the gate that Vince would drive through. Had Spence reached for something when the truck drifted off course, or had he been looking at her in the rearview mirror?

Did it matter?

Yes, her small voice assured her. *It does.*

She was a different person than she'd been a decade ago, and when people like Spence Keller noticed the change—commented on it, even—it gave her a sense of achievement. The discomfort involved in confronting her issues had been worth it. Not that she needed affirmations. People were going to judge; that was a given. But she could accept or reject the judgement. Or ignore it. She could do whatever she wanted with it. She didn't need to change or hide or dodge social events. She could be herself without apology.

For the most part.

She was, like everyone, a work in progress. Had been since she'd made the decision to do something about her shyness on her nineteenth birthday after Jerod, her stepfather du jour, had made yet another joke about her looks improving with age. Instead of swallowing the insult for the umpteenth time, her inner ranch girl—the one who worked shoulder to shoulder with her dad and had skills that stupid Jerod couldn't begin to appreciate—made a surprise appearance and told the man to take a flying leap. Except that what she'd really said had been more colorful, and involved an act that was physically impossible. Hayley could still conjure up the stunned expressions on her mom's and Jerod's faces and the equally stunned silence that followed.

Even though she'd had trouble breathing after blurting out her retort, she hadn't melted into a puddle. She hadn't spontaneously combusted. She'd spoken her mind and she was still in one piece. Reaction had followed revelation, and she'd apologized, because that was what she did to make people back off, but she hadn't meant a word of it.

That had been the second in a long string of realizations. Why say things that she didn't mean just to be left alone? Why not stand up for herself and not back down?

Why look for approval from others?

Because she'd been conditioned to do that.

So she began to get unconditioned. She'd been shocked when her therapist suggested that her glamorous multi-wed mom might be insecure. At first, she'd laughed it off. Reba Summers? Insecure? Nonsense. This guy didn't know her mother. If he did, he would be dazzled by her like everyone else.

But as the sessions continued, she began to understand what the counselor had been getting at. Began to see that her mom had been ill-equipped to be a parent and the wisest thing Hayley had ever done was to insist on moving in with her father at the age of eleven. The second wisest was to seek counseling.

Putting herself out there, risking rejection, accepting criticism, had been daunting, but when the need to retreat began to overwhelm her, she'd conjured up images of Jerod calling her mousy, and David, her stepfather before that, joking about inheriting the proverbial redheaded stepchild, a sentiment that had caused her to feel bad about her hair for years.

She loved her hair now.

She also felt tons more comfortable in her skin.

She smiled down at the little dog. "So you made a break for it, eh? I bet your new mom is worried about you."

Vince Gilroy pulled the open-topped Jeep to a stop and bailed out over the closed door. "Is that Greta?" he asked before pushing up his wire-rimmed glasses, which tended to slip.

"It is."

"Did they turn her in again?"

"I think she left of her own accord. Spence Keller found her near his place and dropped her off."

Vince ruffled the fur on the dog's neck and was rewarded with a few canine kisses. "What now?"

"I'll call Whiskers and Paw Pals, the shelter in Marietta, and let them know what happened. They can handle the rest on their end."

"Going to foster her in the meantime?"

Hayley gave a soft snort. "Of course." She halfway wished she'd never let the little sweetheart go, but she had to in order to foster the next needy dog, who'd turned out to be an overgrown potbelly pig. Remy the Pig had been on the Lone Tree Ranch for two weeks and had claimed Vince as her own shortly after she arrived, nosing along behind him wherever he went.

A second later a loud squeal announced the black-and-white pig's joy at seeing her soulmate. She trotted across the driveway, her curly tail wiggling as she made a beeline for Vince.

Vince, who had declared himself to be neither a cat nor dog man, was now a pig man, whether he liked it or not.

"Hello, beautiful," he said as he reached down to scratch the pig's bristly back. Remy snorted and wiggled. He smiled down at the pig, but the smile faded as he straightened, pushed up his glasses, and met Hayley's gaze.

"I heard back," he said simply.

"When do you leave?"

Because she'd always assumed that her brilliant, dorky ranch hand was going to be accepted into law school at the University of Montana, even though he'd been wait-listed.

"Sooner than expected because I also nailed down the internship. Two calls in a row. I have a few things I have to take care of before I can leave." He started talking faster, his excitement beginning to show. "Finding a place to live, stuff like that."

"Good thing you're a city boy, so there'll be no culture shock." Vince had come to the Lone Tree Ranch from the Bay Area during the summer of his junior year in high school. His father and Hayley's had been friends, and Vince's dad thought his son could use a break from academia. Vince, who'd been hesitant about physical labor and the outdoors, had discovered that he loved ranch work as much as he loved studying. Since that time, he'd spent every summer on the ranch, and when Hayley's father passed away shortly after he'd earned his bachelor's degree, he'd settled on the ranch to help Hayley on a more permanent basis. But they'd both known that he was not meant to be a full-time ranch hand, much as he loved the life.

"Once I pass the bar exam, I'll be back here, practicing law in my adopted hometown." He gave her a half smile. "I assume that Remy will have a home here until I come back?"

"So you're making it official? You and Remy, I mean."

"Only if you agree to watch her for me."

"You might be able to find a place in Missoula that allows pets," she said in a deadpan voice.

"I think I'd rather have Remy than roommates, but I don't see her coming up with her share of the rent every month."

"Touché." Hayley started for the house and Vince fell into step. "I'm proud of you."

"I hate leaving you in a lurch."

"Connor and Ash will be here next week," she reminded him. The two high school kids who worked for the ranch from the end of May to late August when school started again.

"Then you'd best get them to work on the fences or the cows are going to walk through them."

"I'll get right on it."

Vince grinned. "You do that."

"Stop bossing."

"Look who's talking."

Hayley gave a mock cough. "The boss."

Chapter Two

THE DOOR TO the three-room homestead house, built in 1910 by Spence's great-great-grandfather, creaked in classic haunted house style as Spence pushed it open. When he stepped into the small living area, the musty scent of abandonment hit his nostrils and he wrinkled his nose. "I'll stay in the main house."

"After all the work the folks have done to keep it rodent free? Come on." Reed, Spence's older brother, followed him inside the hundred-year-old dwelling. "Perfect guesthouse."

No. It had been the perfect playhouse for Em and Cade, who'd claimed it as their own years ago. The lack of insulation and the outdated fixtures and plumbing made it a not-so-perfect guesthouse. The only reason it was still standing was because Em loved it and when the roof had started to go, Daniel had chosen to replace it rather than bulldoze the place as common sense decreed. He had a hard time saying no to his only daughter.

"Come on—it's perfect," Reed said in an encouraging voice.

"So sayeth the guy with running water and electricity."

His brother occupied the house their grandparents had lived in, next door to the main ranch house, while Spence was currently living in the main house. He would have claimed the second bedroom in the little house, but Reed's fifteen-year-old daughter, Lex, stayed there when she visited from Bozeman where she lived with her mom and stepdad.

Reed grinned at him. "You, too, can have those amenities. It'll just take a few days to hook them up."

Spence shook his head. "Not being a prima donna or anything, but—"

"You're totally a prima donna."

"But I think I will continue in the folks' house. I don't know how long I'll be here, and I don't have a lot of spare cash to sink into this place." He was pretty certain that the old wiring and delicate plumbing system would present a whole nest of new problems if they were put into use.

"That I understand."

Spence was remarkably debt free because he didn't sink money into things that didn't give a decent return, and when he had debt, he paid it off as quickly as possible. He owned his truck and the travel trailer he lived in on locations if his expenses weren't covered by his contract, which they usually were. He had enough money in the bank to meet his needs for several months—actually, for more than a year if he was frugal—and he planned on rustling up some welding jobs while he was in the area. But he was not going to sink capital into a rundown homestead house when his mom assured him that she loved having him in his old bedroom. It would have been better if it wasn't now her sewing room, but in the few days he'd been home, they'd managed to work around one another.

"Can you still ride?" Reed asked as they stepped out of the homestead house.

"What kind of question is that?" Spence hooked the hasp that served as a secondary lock to the place.

"When's the last time you were on a horse?"

"I can outride you."

"We'll see about that tomorrow." When they planned to ride the allotment fence prior to turning out the cattle.

"Yeah." Spence lifted a hand to shade his eyes as he studied the dust plume rising behind the truck that barreled into sight where the driveway emerged from the tree line. "I'd say Dad has something on his mind."

"Shit." Reed propped his hands on his hips. "I was hoping that we were done with this crap."

Spence watched his brother's face tighten. Reed was engaged to Trenna Hunt, the daughter of the guy who was raising hell with the family in an attempt to gain right-of-way across their best hay field in order to build a resort on the mountainside. Spence couldn't say that the family was wild about the idea of having a resort looking down on the ranch, but they could accept it, mainly because they had no choice. Hunt owned the land. What they couldn't accept was a barrage of traffic traveling across their fields on their way to

Hunt's resort. Carter Hunt had another option to access the property, but it involved building a bridge across the deep V of a narrow rocky canyon called Robber's Gorge. That option would be wildly expensive, so Hunt continued his quest to get the Kellers to bow to his wishes.

Daniel Keller and family were not prone to bowing.

By the time the truck pulled to a stop, Reed and Spence were waiting by the barn. To Spence's surprise, Henry Still Smoking, their longtime ranch hand who was supposed to retire, but didn't seem able to get the job done, was at the wheel. The normally easygoing guy looked as pissed off as Daniel, which was saying something.

Daniel Keller grimaced as he worked his way out of the truck. He'd had back surgery a few years ago, and now he was looking at another round to fuse the vertebrae about those that were already fused. The price of ranch work, the surgeon had said.

Indeed. Ranch work, coupled with stubbornness and a refusal to accept that he might have to change his ways. The prospect of the second surgery had slowed him down a bit, but Spence couldn't help wondering if his dad would be right back at it once he healed a second time.

But with Reed home, and Henry reluctant to pull the plug, Spence figured his time at the ranch would be over in the early fall. Once winter set it, there wasn't much to do beyond feeding cattle, which Reed could handle.

"What happened?" Reed asked Henry, giving their dad a

chance to regain his composure after the pain of getting out of the rig.

"That asshole found a loophole to shut off the irrigation to the east fields."

"We're junior water rights holders by one year," Daniel explained. "One year. And since Hunt has been using that right in a piddling way, he's kept it. Now he plans to pretty much drain the canal before it reaches us."

"What if he gets to put a road across the field?" Spence asked.

"I imagine his water usage would revert to normal," Daniel said grimly. "Meanwhile, the field dries up."

WHAT WAS SHE going to do without Vince?

Hayley's stomach began knotting while she helped pack and load his truck. Vince's acceptance into law school had been something of a long shot this year and with the labor market being tight, she'd hoped that he'd get into law school next year.

Selfish wish. She should have worked harder at a backup plan, but in reality, how? It seemed unlikely that she could have found someone to wait in the wings just in case Vince got the call he'd been waiting for.

Tonight she'd post on social media to see if she could find additional help for the summer. The situation wasn't dire. She and Connor and Ash could handle the work, but she needed a second come fall when the boys went back to school. She could use a second right now to help with the general workload—especially now that she was developing the farmer's market side gig. That was for personal satisfaction, and it could slide, but she'd just gotten her greenhouse and was excited to start production.

"That's it, boss." Vince came out of the duplex cottage, pulling the door shut behind him. Remy snuffled at his pant leg, and he bent down to rub her ears. "I think I'll put her away and say goodbye," he said.

Hayley nodded and watched as Vince pulled a carrot out of his shirt pocket and called the pig to the yard, where he gave her the carrot before locking the gate. "She can't chase me now."

"Unless she digs under the gate."

"I'll be gone." Vince gave Hayley a long look and she could see how torn he was about leaving.

"It's not like I'm never going to see you again. And who knows? Maybe I'll need a lawyer."

"Are you kidding? I plan on being on retainer once I pass the bar."

"That you will," Hayley said before opening her arms and giving him a hug. "Thank you for staying with me after Dad died," she said. He could have headed back to Missoula then and gotten a better-paying job while he waited to hear about law school, but instead he'd stayed and helped her run the ranch while she grieved her father's passing. She was forever grateful and, although she'd known this day was coming, it was so much harder to deal with than she'd anticipated.

Her throat felt thick, and she swallowed. Vince looked like he was also on the edge of emotion, and Vince didn't do emotions, so Hayley stepped back. "Keep in contact, visit often, and consider spending Christmas here."

Vince laughed. "Will do. Thanks, boss. Take care of my sweetheart for me until I have a place that I can keep her."

"Will do."

Remy, sensing that the love of her life wasn't returning anytime soon, squealed and ran the fence as Vince drove away. Then she stood watching through the slats as the truck disappeared.

"We're on our own," Hayley said to the pig as she let herself into the front yard. Remy ignored her, continuing to watch through the slats.

Vince had done her a favor by staying, and now she was doing him a favor by not needing him. She'd sidestepped his questions about how she planned to replace him, and he stopped asking after the third try. She'd manage because that was what she did.

Hayley let Greta out of the house, and the little terrier trotted across the lawn to stand next to Remy as the pig stared down the driveway. If Greta needed a new foster home, Hayley would once again volunteer. Remy needed a friend. Hayley found her phone and was searching for the number to Whiskers and Paw Pals when a call came in.

"Mom. Hi."

She'd been taught from a young age to call her mom Reba when they were around people, but in the privacy of her kitchen, she could call her mother anything she liked. And she liked Mom. That was what her kid was going to call her. That or Mama. She wasn't picky as long as she wasn't referred to as Hayley.

"Hi, sweetie." Reba's voice was low and husky. Hayley had long admired her mom's voice modulation. "I just wanted to touch base before leaving."

"Thanks, Mom." She'd been through this procedure too many times to ask, "Are you sure about this?" Because her mother would indicate that she was passionately certain that this guy was the one and yes, heading off for a multi-month tour of South Pacific islands was the perfect way to spend the summer. A week here, a week there. Exactly the way Reba liked to live life, and the exact opposite of how Hayley liked to live, another reason she'd moved to the Lone Tree.

The important thing was that Reba was happy, and, thanks to her lawyer, who was actually husband number two after Hayley's dad, her assets were tied up in a way that it was hard for a new beau to get at. Not that Reba would let them. She loved to fall in love, but she also liked to live well, and she was not about to risk the latter for the former.

"I'll be out of the country for two, maybe three, months,

but I promise that the second I get back into the States, I'll visit."

"That would be nice, Mom."

They chatted for several more minutes about superficial things because that was what they were comfortable with. They'd never shared mother-daughter secrets, nor had Hayley wanted to. She'd realized from a young age that her mom wasn't like other moms, and by the time she'd moved in with her dad, she'd been comfortable having one 'normal' parent. Her other parent, her mom, was like an elusive butterfly. Beautiful and charming, she'd flit in and out of Hayley's life, and because that was the only relationship Hayley had known with her mother, she'd accepted it—for the most part. Sometimes she envied her friends with two normal parents, and at other times, when she had friends dealing with strife in their families, she was glad her parents had figured things out so early. She remembered no fights between her mom and dad because she'd been so young when they split up. By the time she was aware of their interactions, they'd developed a distant, yet amiable, relationship for her sake. So, no full-time mom, but no upheavals, either.

By her late teens, she'd come to understand that if her mom hadn't accidentally become pregnant with her, she wouldn't have had children at all. Reba was open about having her tubes tied after Hayley's birth, and equally open about her diagnosis of endometriosis in her early thirties, which had caused her to have a partial hysterectomy. Ironically, like her own mother, Reba had fertility issues, but had still managed an accidental pregnancy.

Hayley was hoping to do the same, but without the accident part.

Hayley wished her mom a safe trip, didn't let on that she couldn't remember the name of the current beau—John, Jean, Jean-Ralphio, something like that—and then hung up with the usual empty feeling that followed a call with her sole parent. Now that her dad was gone, she realized that she wanted a *mom* mom. She didn't have one. But . . . she could be one. And she was going to.

After hanging up, she ambled down the hallway to the room next to her bedroom. The room that had once been her dad's, which she was turning into a kid's room. She hadn't done much yet because she was half-afraid of jinxing herself and never having a kid. It appeared that time was not on her side.

Hayley was almost twenty-nine and when her last visit to the doctor had indicated that she, too, was in the early stages of developing endometriosis, she'd decided to act. Unlike her mother, she wanted children, which meant doing something before her body began working against her. There were many avenues to achieve that goal, and she may well try them all, but to begin with, she was going with the old-fashioned way.

Well, maybe not old-fashioned, since it involved medical intervention.

She leaned against the doorjamb and studied the room, which she'd painted a delicious pale green and trimmed with white. Good start. She'd had meetings with counseling personnel at the clinic she'd chosen, and now it was a matter of picking a father from the fine catalog they had on hand, and deciding when to start Operation Baby.

She was thinking late fall, after the fields had been harvested and the ground turned over and the cattle brought in. The big question was how long it would take to get pregnant via artificial insemination—after she chose a father, of course. That was another issue slowing her down. That damned catalog with all those guys staring back at her. What if she chose wrong?

They're vetted. The clinic has a stellar rep.

True. And it wasn't like she was going to go cruising for a baby daddy in person. That wasn't her style. She might have come out of her shell, but not to that degree. The catalog it was.

Hayley pushed off the doorjamb and closed the door. The house was quiet, too quiet sometimes, reminding her that her dad was gone, but despite the silence, the house had a good feel. She'd put hours and hours into making it cozy after returning home from college, and she loved everything about it, from the sunny kitchen to the colorful throw pillows she'd made last winter.

Funny thing, she thought, as she lit the burner beneath the teakettle—she was never without a project or goal. In high school, she'd been driven to become valedictorian. She'd ended up salutatorian, but she could live with that. When she went to college, she'd graduated cum laude with a degree that was actually pretty useless in a practical sense, though she didn't regret her course of study. Going to college had broadened her perspective and better prepared her for parenthood. And now she was pouring her energies into making the ranch a real home and having a baby. Making the best of the life she had.

She only wished that her dad could have been there to be a grandfather to the child. He would have been the best grandpa . . .

Hayley blinked the sting away from her eyes and focused on matters she did have control of. Running the ranch. She needed help in that regard, so tomorrow, when she took Greta to Whiskers and Paw Pals, she'd ask around, see if anyone knew of a reliable person looking for ranch work.

"It's okay, Grandpa." Lex, Reed's fifteen-year-old daughter, grinned over her shoulder. "I know that word too."

She might know the word, but Spence wished his dad would watch his tongue.

Lex made a show of closing the dishwasher, twisting the knob to start it, then dusting off her hands. "I'll just head next door so that you can speak freely."

"Thank you." Daniel's voice sounded a touch choked, but he maintained a straight face. He waited until Lex had grabbed her sweatshirt and headed out the door before repeating the word he shouldn't have said in front of his granddaughter.

Spence's mom, Audrey, set an affectionate hand on her husband's shoulder. "Well said," she murmured without a hint of irony.

"I think it sums up the situation," Reed said. "Now we need a solution."

Daniel put his hands on the table in front of him, tucking his thumbs under the edge. "Last time we had a water issue, you guys were little, so you probably don't remember."

"No," Spence said. "We do." The issues the drought had caused had been hard to miss. The canal had dried up and fields on the east side of the ranch had gone yellow after only one cutting of alfalfa. On the west side, however, they'd managed two more cuttings, thanks to being able to pump leased water and continue irrigating.

He met his dad's gaze, realizing where this was going. "You got water from the Lone Tree Ranch." Their nearest neighbor and the most water-rich ranch in the valley.

"And hope to do it again. The thing is that Old Darrell was still alive at the time, and I dealt with him. Now both Darrell and Hank"—Hayley's grandfather and dad—"are gone, which might complicate matters."

"Because you don't know Hanna?" Reed asked.

"Hayley," Spence corrected. "Her name is Hayley."

"Yeah. Sorry," Reed said.

"Hayley," Daniel repeated. "I only recognize her because of her hair. No, I don't know her."

"I know her," Spence said.

"You know her?" Reed asked. "How? You left home before she graduated and as near as I can tell, you haven't spent much time back here."

"I know her from high school." Reed cocked his head in a disbelieving way, and Spence explained. "We had an encounter."

Audrey lifted her hands as if to ward off what he was about to say next.

"She saved my ass," Spence said.

"When? How?" Reed scowled at Spence.

"I was a senior, and this is going to sound kind of stupid now, but you remember Lucas Barstow?"

"That mountain?" Reed said. "Kind of hard to forget him. What happened?"

"I might have run my mouth at him once too often, and before the bus left for the championship basketball game, he locked me in the equipment shed. You know Coach's rules back then. If you're not dressed out by warmups, you're not playing." And even though he'd been a top scorer, the coach would have kept his word.

"Hayley heard me pounding and managed to let me out. Then she drove me to the game." He decided to leave the part out about the cop stopping them. "We passed the bus, and I was waiting there when it arrived." He smiled reminiscently. "You should have seen the look on Barstow's face when he saw me leaning against the lamppost as the bus drove up."

"Hayley Parker. Red hair. Braids. Glasses. That Hayley Parker."

"She'd lost the braids by then. Still had glasses." He'd been impressed at how coolly she'd handled matters. "I'll get you to the game," she'd said matter-of-factly. And then she did.

"You owe her a favor," Daniel said.

"Yeah. I do." Plus, he hadn't properly thanked her for rescuing his sorry ass. "But I think that I might be the guy to talk to her about this situation."

"I don't know," Audrey said slowly. "Maybe your dad should."

Daniel met Spence's gaze. "Spence?"

"I'll do it." He owed Hayley, and he had an idea as to how to repay her, which might tip a decision as to water in their favor. Or maybe the money they'd pay would do that.

"I need details," he said. "How much water did we lease, what did we pay then, and what's a fair rate now?"

Audrey pushed back from the table. "I'll get you that information."

His mom was one of the most organized people he knew, which was why the Keller Ranch ran so smoothly. A few minutes later, she returned with a manila folder, which she opened and placed in front of Daniel.

"This amount of water would see us through," Daniel said after reviewing the contract. "We only need to irrigate the fields bordering the Hunt property. This time the west side is good." Being fed, as it was from a different, newly constructed ditch with a different water source. That water could only be used on the west fields, but leased aquifer water could be pumped wherever it was needed.

Spence looked at the figures, then said, "I'll talk to her today."

"Be convincing," Daniel said. "Otherwise, I'm not sure what we can do other than to let that asshole win."

Then they'd have to decide between a major thoroughfare across their property with the associated collateral damage, or watering the field.

Spence knew that Daniel would let the field dry up and blow away before he kowtowed to Carter Hunter; therefore, his mission was clear.

Nail down a lease, regardless of the conditions. Daniel would rather pay through the nose than let "that asshole," Carter Hunt, win.

GRETA LAID HER bristly chin on Hayley's leg as they left Marietta. Hayley settled a protective hand on the dog's warm body as she brought the truck up to speed. She'd intended to drop off the terrier at Whiskers and Paw Pals so that her adoptive mom could pick her up, only to find that the adoptive mom was no longer employed by the Hunt Ranch and couldn't keep Greta until she came up with a new place to live.

"So what did she think she was going to do at the end of the season?" Elena Romero, the shelter manager, asked Hayley. "It drives me crazy when people lie on the applications. She said she was a year-round employee and now we find that she was seasonal, *and* she did not get fired. She quit."

"You're certain?"

"I called out there. Talked to Dawn Hunt herself." Carter Hunt was something of a jerk, but everyone liked his second wife, who participated in many community events and charities. "We need to amp up the vetting situation."

"Along with everything else you do," Hayley had said as she cuddled Greta against her. "And how many failures have you had in the past year?"

Elena looked skyward. "Two."

"Not bad considering the number of animals you've homed. I heard that *someone* took in a potbellied pig."

"It's not a permanent home." Elena made a sad face.

"I think it might turn into one."

Elena's eyes widened. "You're adopting Remy?"

"I think Vince will, after he finishes law school. In the

meantime, she'll live with me."

"Excellent." Elena tilted her head at the little dog. "Care to foster Greta again?"

Hayley rubbed the little dog's ears. "Of course."

"Care to adopt?"

Hayley made a face. "If I start adopting, I'll never stop." And she had no idea how busy she was going to be in the future. "But . . . you never know." If push came to shove, she would indeed adopt the little dog.

Chapter Three

*C*AN I STOP *by to discuss a matter?*

The message had been waiting on her answering machine when Hayley got home. She'd called the Keller Ranch, spoke to Reed, who wasn't forthcoming with details, then agreed to meet Spence that afternoon. She was mystified. What on earth did Spence want to discuss with her? Try as she might, she couldn't come up with anything. Did it have something to do with her telling him that he'd never thanked her properly?

She should have lied and said, "Of course you thanked me."

But he hadn't, and she was surprised that it still kind of dug at her. She hadn't liked being invisible, even if she'd been the one to make herself that way, which was why she was the opposite of invisibility now. She wore her red hair loose instead of tightly confined in braids and twists, and wore bright colors, even if those colors sometimes clashed with her hair. Red and purple were a thing, right? When people looked at her, she looked back without ducking her head, and felt good about it.

She'd overcome shyness—at least to the point where she could fake it if she did suffer an attack—but she was still a little edgy about Spence Keller's upcoming visit. Why?

Probably because she could still recall how he had looked and smelled and filled the cab of her small truck with his presence as they roared down the highway leading to Big Sky for the championship basketball game. Remembered feeling things that she'd never experienced before.

He was your first.

Hayley gave a soft laugh at the ridiculous thought, but in a way, it was true. He was the first guy who'd ever made her feel *that* way. A heady mix of lust and longing and forbidden fruit. She hadn't been confident enough back then to make the first move, but now . . .

Now she didn't need to. She knew what she wanted. Two bad relationships in a row had cured her of the need for a partner thing—a lesson her mother never learned. Hayley loved her mother, but she didn't understand her, and she didn't want to mirror her life. On the rare occasion where Reba did not do the dumping, she'd been able to pick herself up and move on as if nothing had happened.

Hayley envied her mother that ability.

You have your own talents.

She did, at that. And she was happy living on her ranch, planning her future, and being her own boss. What more did she need?

LONE TREE RANCH was a welcoming place, from the whimsical HOWDY sign on the big gate at the cattle guard to the neatly cultivated garden. The Keller Ranch was well maintained, but the Lone Tree had those little touches that made the place seem well cared for and loved. Spence wasn't certain how many people Hayley had working for her, or even what the ranch had looked like before she'd taken over, but he was nevertheless impressed.

He caught a movement in the fenced garden next to the house—it looked like she had three or four gardens—and then Hayley stood and stretched her back before turning at the sound of his truck.

Her long red hair was caught in a loose ponytail, which was partially covered by the hat resting on her back and hanging from a string around her neck. She pushed wispy tendrils of hair back from her forehead as he got out of his truck, then she headed to the garden gate, the little dog dancing at her feet.

"Hi, again," Spence said as he approached the garden, the manila folder with the lease information in one hand. A small rototiller, meant to cultivate between rows, stood near the gate, having obviously just been used.

Hayley tossed a handful of rocks onto the driveway. "Hi," she said, taking off her gloves and jamming the tops into her back pocket. Her gaze strayed briefly to the folder he carried, before coming back to his face. "I'm getting ready to plant. Every year I think I have all the rocks out of the bed and every year I find more."

"Frost heaves." Spence looked past the area where she'd been working to the two identically fenced areas. "You have a lot of gardens."

"Two vegetable, one flower," she said. "And the greenhouse."

"Where?"

"Behind the barn. It's new this year. Well, this week actually. I'm pretty excited."

"You must really be into fresh food."

"And farmer's markets."

"Yeah?"

"I was a regular in Livingston, but this year, Marietta is starting their own market, so I'll be participating there instead."

"It's a little closer."

"And I have friends there."

"Can I see your greenhouse?"

He was buying a little time before getting down to business, but truth be told, he was curious. His mom had talked about getting a greenhouse, but most of her spare time—not that she had a lot—went toward documenting the history of the ranch and the Kellers in the area. That was how Trenna Hunt came into the picture, since archival work was her specialty, and that was how his brother became engaged to the daughter of their family's greatest pain in the ass. Carter Hunt did not approve, but his daughter simply did not care. She loved Reed. Full stop.

What would that be like?

Spence shoved the odd thought out of his head. He and Hayley walked around the corner of the barn, past the half-finished pipe corral. Once they rounded the corner, he could see that a series of corrals had been laid out, plus an area that looked to be a loading chute.

"Big plans?"

"Dad had big plans. They slowed down when he got ill, then eventually ground to a halt. I haven't decided what to do, yet. I mean, the corrals aren't that far along, so maybe I should sell the pipe and continue to depend on the old wooden corrals. They work."

He'd seen the corrals driving in. They were the only part of the Lone Tree Ranch that had a shabby look to them.

"How many cows are you running?"

"Around a hundred. I cut back after Dad passed away."

"That's still quite a few."

"It keeps me busy," she said in a noncommittal way, then pointed at the greenhouse, a prefab building that looked to be perhaps twelve feet wide and sixteen or eighteen feet long. Good sized. Made of some kind of plastic panels set in metal.

"Did you order this online?"

"I did." She opened the door and stood back so that Spence could step inside. "A crew came and set it up for me.

Next year I'm hoping to get an early start on my plants, and once I get the building anchored down, I'll plant some of my tomatoes in here and hopefully have enough to sell at the farmer's market toward the end of summer."

"You're not anchored?"

Anchors were a must on small buildings in the windy country in which they lived.

"I've got the cables. Vince was going to set the anchors for me." She didn't mention the part about him no longer being around to do that. She'd set her own anchors—that evening, if things worked out. She might have to consult YouTube, but she'd get the job done.

"Vince?"

"My ranch guy. He's heading off to law school soon." Like yesterday.

"Summer law school?"

"His internship starts early."

Spence pushed his hat back. "Your ranch hand is a law student."

"He wasn't until a few days ago. Now he is."

"So you need help around the place."

"No. I have two high school kids set to start work as soon as school lets out, and I'm pretty certain I'll get someone permanent nailed down by the end of the summer. Until then, the kids and I can handle stuff." She pushed her hands into her back pockets. "Enough about me."

"You want to know why I'm here."

"You don't appear to have found another dog."

"I have not."

Hayley pushed the back of her wrist over her forehead. "You want some lemonade or iced tea?"

"Sure."

Hayley's house reflected the same homey, yet whimsical, vibe as the rest of the property. The old cupboards were a cheery yellow, and the walls a pale aqua, giving the room a light feeling that Spence appreciated. He took a seat at the oak table, after indicating that he'd like iced tea instead of lemonade, and managed to stop his fingers from tapping out a nervous rhythm on top of the envelope he'd set on the table in front of him.

He had this. But when Hayley sat opposite him and planted her elbows on the table, obviously waiting for him to launch into the reason he'd come, he found himself at something of a loss.

Finally, he said, "Do you remember the drought of 2004?"

"I was ten, maybe? I remember issues with water, but other than that . . ." She made a gesture. "Why?"

"Your dad leased water to us that year. We were wondering if you would be willing to do the same. Since you have Department of Natural Resources approval, you could do it again."

"It's not a drought year."

"It is if the guy above us on the canal decides to use more

water than he ever has before."

"The Hunt Ranch?"

"It's a long story, but our water rights are junior to the Hunt property, so if they want to use all the water, they can. And, apparently, they are."

"Why would they do that to you?"

"They want something we have." He smiled a little. "And because of that, we want something that you have."

"What does Carter Hunt want from you guys?"

Spence outlined the situation with Hunt wanting to build a road across their fields for access to a resort he wanted to build on the mountain.

"Does he have the permits he needs to do that?"

"The zoning is correct, so I imagine a guy like Hunt can get whatever he needs to proceed." Spence sipped his lemonade. "He tried to take over the land through adverse possession. That situation is still brewing, and made all the more complicated because Reed is dating Trenna Hunt."

"Wow. Soap opera stuff."

"It is for a guy who just wants to live in peace."

"Who's that guy?"

"Me."

Her laugh bubbled up and Hayley quickly pressed her fingers to her lips. "Sorry."

Spence scowled at her. "What?"

"You were not a guy who sought out peace."

"Maybe I was hiding that side of myself," he said softly.

"Kind of like you were hiding part of yourself." She lifted her eyebrows and he said, "You didn't talk. As near as I could tell, you actively worked to be invisible."

"Good point." But she didn't look convinced that he was a guy in search of a peaceful existence. He was. Whereas Reed still had to fight the occasional wild impulse, Spence was happy embracing the moment.

He put the glass down on a pamphlet sitting near him on the table to avoid making a water ring with the damp glass. "What do you think about leasing water?"

Hayley's gaze had followed his glass, but now it jerked up to his. "I need to look into the matter. See what was done in 2004, and what can be done now."

"I have copies of the paperwork from the original deal." He opened the envelope and pulled out a thin sheath of papers. "We're looking at almost the exact same situation as far as amount of water and length of lease."

Hailey scanned the top page, then looked at him from beneath her lashes. "I imagine the price has gone up."

He smiled. "That's something we need to talk about. Dad and I put some figures together. Just turn the page."

Hayley did so, studying the numbers Spence had written out because Daniel's handwriting was so atrocious, then leaned back in her chair. "Leave this and I'll run it by my lawyer."

"I'd appreciate it if you'd do that." More than anything, he wanted an instant yes, but that wasn't going to happen, nor had he expected it to. "We need the water, Hayley. Soon."

"Ken will give me a quick answer. He's an old friend of Dad's."

"Ken Willard?"

Hayley nodded, and Spence felt a whisper of relief. Ken was a Matlock-type guy, very experienced and trustworthy.

"I wish I could say yes right now, but . . ."

"I totally get it, Hayley." A business needed to be run with logic, not emotions.

"Good."

She met his gaze, looking grateful for his understanding, and Spence was momentarily distracted by the color of her eyes, moss green with gold around the irises. He'd stared into them through her glasses the night she'd rescued him and recalled how he'd been struck by the color back then too.

He picked up his glass and the pamphlet he'd set it on stuck to the damp bottom. It dropped to the table and Spence read the title. *AI vs. IVF: What You Need to Know.*

His first thought was that Hayley was either AI—artificially inseminating—cattle or implanting fertilized embryos in them, both of which were common practices in the beef industry. But when he glanced up and saw that her face had gone cherry red, he realized that he might have stumbled onto something more personal. A quick glance at the pamphlet cover showed a smiling woman with a baby. Not a cow in sight. Oh yeah. Definitely not a can of worms to be opened.

"Tell me about the Farmer's Market in Marietta," he said in a voice that sounded a tad too smooth.

Hayley smiled weakly and lifted her lemonade glass. Her cheeks were still burning.

"Saturday mornings, nine to one, starting next week. There won't be much in the way of produce until later in the summer, so artisans and handcrafters will have to carry things until then. I'm going to sell seedlings from my greenhouse and cut flowers until my produce is ready." She smiled down at Greta. "I can also show off my foster animals and see if anyone is interested."

Hayley's gaze strayed to the pamphlet as if she wished she could make it disappear.

Spence had mercy. He set the glass on the pamphlet, covering most of the title, then pushed his chair back. "I should be going."

Hayley got to her feet. "I'll be in touch," she said as she walked him to the door. Her cheeks were still pink, but her expression was now impassive.

"Thanks." He gave her a quick smile.

Hayley had recovered from her embarrassment, so there was no reason for Spence to feel self-conscious as he headed down the front walkway to his truck. But he did.

If Hayley was looking into fertility treatments, that was none of his business. For all he knew, she had a significant other and they were looking at having kids. Or perhaps she was researching the matter for other reasons.

None of his business.

HE'S GONE. NOW you can curl up and die.

Hayley gave herself a mental shake. If she was going to embark on this journey of single parenthood, people were going to notice. And she, the person who still fought the occasional battle against shyness and self-consciousness despite everything, was going to have to woman-up and face it. She picked up the pamphlet from the table and after a last look—she had the information memorized—she tossed it into the trash, where it could cause her no more difficulties.

Now the water lease.

She wished her dad was there so that she could question him about what happened the last time he'd leased water. Instead, she called Ken to discuss the matter. He wasn't in, so she left a message, then pulled the gloves from her back pocket. She had to finish turning over her garden, and then anchor her greenhouse if she wanted to keep it on the property. Winds in the area tended to move untethered buildings to new locations.

Greta danced at the door, waiting for Hayley to open it, and just outside, Remy waited in hopes of Vince magically appearing. The pig was going to miss her top ranch hand.

Hayley headed off to the garden, dog and pig following

close behind. She had a decent fence, so both dog and pig stayed outside as she started the rototiller. Her cold weather plants were producing, and the tomatoes in her greenhouse were already budding, so she'd have fare for the Farmer's Market.

She finished turning over the part of the garden she would plant tomorrow, then secured the canvas cover over the rototiller, lashing it extra tight so the wind didn't blow it off. While she worked, she'd debated pros and cons of leasing water to the Kellers, and frankly, couldn't come up with a con. She'd get money, and water would get used, so if there were no legal issues, she'd lease the water to the Kellers. They were good neighbors and her father had been friendly with Daniel, the patriarch of the family.

Her quiet dad hadn't had much in common with Daniel Keller, but he had told stories about the man's exploits when they'd gone to high school together. Reed Keller, the oldest son, had taken after his father. That said, Spence was also an adventurer, but in a quieter, less in-your-face way. Beneath that laid-back exterior was a guy looking for a good time. While Reed grabbed the bad boy spotlight, Spence managed to operate relatively unnoticed.

But Hayley had noticed.

THE WIND RATTLED the house, intensifying the sense of

restlessness that dogged Spence during storms. He'd never done well with the wind, while his younger sister, Em, embraced it. She said it was genetic memory from their seafaring Viking ancestors. He said that she was nuts. She'd simply smiled. Em was a Viking at heart.

He was a guy who hated windstorms.

At least all the trees close enough to buildings to do serious damage had been trimmed recently, so unless one of the roofs peeled off from a building, there was no reason not to kick back, put in earplugs and continue reading.

Except that the image of Hayley Parker's not-yet-anchored greenhouse kept creeping into his brain.

How was it faring in this wind?

He walked through the empty house—his folks were on an overnight trip to Bozeman for medical tests prior to his dad's surgery—and grabbed the phone book from the cookbook stand. There was no listing for Hayley Parker, or even for her late father, but there was a listing for the Lone Tree Ranch.

He called the number, and it rang until a mechanical voice came onto the line, informing him that the party's mailbox had yet to be set up.

Spence hung up the phone and stared out the window at the trees bending in the wind. It wasn't yet twilight, although the storm had darkened the sky as if it were, so why not take a drive over and see how things were faring? If Hayley's ranch hand was still away, and if Spence had understood her correctly, the guy should still be in Missoula, then she was dealing with the greenhouse alone—and she might be doing that right now, since she hadn't answered. Or she might not be home at all.

Yeah. No harm in a fifteen-minute drive to make certain everything was okay. He might not have stopped by to say hello, or to have thanked her properly for saving his ass, but he could do this.

The wind lifted Spence's hat as he stepped out the door. He caught it and then tossed it onto the truck seat a few seconds later. The lights were on in the little house where Reed lived, but Spence didn't bother telling his brother he was taking off. He hadn't answered to anyone except for himself and his bosses for such a long time that the idea was kind of foreign.

He drove around a tree branch that partially blocked the county road, feeling more justified in his decision to check on the woman from whom he was asking a major favor. Yes, it might look like he was kissing ass, but he'd hate it if he didn't check, and something happened.

When Spence pulled into the driveway of the Lone Tree Ranch, the place was dark, with the exception of occasional glimmers of light from beneath the barn's double bay doors.

No power, obviously, so the light was probably from Hayley checking things in the barn. He stopped the truck, left the headlights on, and made his way to the barn door. There was no way to make his presence known without startling the shit out of Hayley, short of sitting in his truck and waiting for her to come out, and he was debating how to announce himself when the barn door opened and Hayley poked her head out, squinting at his headlights. He got out of his truck, ducking his head against the wind that ripped at his denim jacket. Hailey stepped back to allow him into the barn, then pushed the door shut against the wind, the beam from the flashlight she held arcing over the ground near her feet. Her face was barely illuminated when she turned toward him, but he could still read confusion.

"Spence. What are you doing here?"

"I remembered that you said your greenhouse wasn't anchored down."

"It is now," she said. "I got the wind advisory a few hours ago and got to work cabling it to the ground." The wind beat on the door like a battering ram, but Hayley didn't seem one bit bothered. "Did you drive over to *check* on me?"

Spence felt warmth creep up his neck at her disbelieving tone. "I was worried about the greenhouse. I called the ranch number and got no answer. I thought you could use a hand."

"I see." The direction of her thoughts was obvious, even in the dim light.

He shifted his weight under her scrutiny. "I know it looks like I'm being extra-attentive after asking for a massive favor."

"Well, I have seen you three times in less than three days after not seeing you for years."

51

He smiled at her justifiably wary observation.

"That does look suspicious, but I promise you that I have no ulterior motive. You're on my radar because of the dog and the water lease, but I'm not trying to sway you." One corner of his mouth quirked up. "I would if I could, but that wasn't my intention."

"So if the water issue was settled, you would be here anyway?"

"Now that I know you live alone here on the ranch, yes." Spence wasn't used to having neighbors, but when he did, in RV parks and trailer camps and such, he was glad to lend a hand if needed. He would have worried about the wind and the greenhouse, and he would have driven over to check.

She gave him a thoughtful look, and he found himself studying the lines of her face as he waited for her to speak. Hayley Parker had grown into one attractive woman.

"The greenhouse is cabled down, and unless a branch or a tree falls on the house, all is well here."

"I'm dismissed?"

"I appreciate your coming over. It was . . . nice." Her mouth tilted ruefully. "I didn't mean to sound dismissive."

"Even though I've been dismissed."

"Pretty much. I have everything under control."

"You have no electricity," he pointed out.

"Can you fix that?" she asked innocently.

Spence had to smile, and Hayley's lips twitched before she said, "I have candles and lanterns. I'm fine."

She was also in command of the situation, and he was not. Interesting turn.

Hayley unlatched the door and it whipped open, slamming against the wall of the barn. She winced at the noise, then said, "You'd better get home before a tree comes down on the road."

Spence stepped out into the wind and waited while Hayley latched the barn door, turning his head against the roar of the wind.

"I'll be in contact," she yelled.

He nodded and then walked around his truck and got inside, taking care not to let the wind rip the door out of his hand and damage the hinges. Hayley was already on her way to her house, the beam of the flashlight bobbing on the ground in front of her. She stopped at the gate, apparently waiting for him to drive away, which he did, masterfully missing the gatepost.

But he had to admit he really hated to go. Hated to leave her there alone.

And that might be something to think about. Was it the past or present that gave him the feeling that this new Hayley was getting under his skin?

Chapter Four

AFTER MEETING WITH Ken Willard and catching him up on the ranch happenings and assuring him that she was doing well, Hayley learned that there was nothing to stop her from leasing water to the Kellers if she so chose.

The Lone Tree Ranch, her ranch, was one of the oldest on that side of the valley, and had both surface and subsurface water rights. Because she had fields laying fallow that year, it was the perfect time to lease—and the money from the lease would be useful for her baby project.

Ken started drawing up the paperwork, promising to have it ready the next day, and Hayley walked down the street and around the corner from his offices to grab a cup of coffee with her old friend and fellow geek, Bella Knight, who'd moved back to Marietta a few months ago.

Hayley spotted Bella's dark curls, and she would have waved, except that Bella's nose was deep in her book. She looked up as Hayley approached, then pushed her glasses up, reminding her of Vince, which caused a pang.

"I'm at the good part."

It was a joke they'd shared since high school, when

they'd both rather read than participate in whatever was going on around them. A survival skill at the time. They looked studious, which in turn had people giving them a wide berth.

"I'm sure you are." Hayley sat as the server cruised by with the coffeepot. He held up the pot, both Bella and Hayley nodded, and a second later, Hayley was dumping a small container of half-and-half into the dark brew.

"Are you settling into your new place?" Hayley asked before lifting her cup. Bella had just purchased a small house— a cottage, really—on the edge of town, having taken a job at the local clinic.

Bella pushed her book aside. "I'm making progress. I have a three-day break coming up. I'll be painting when I'm not sleeping." She leaned her elbows on the table. "Before you offer to help, because I know how much you *love* painting, I'm taking my time, enjoying audiobooks while I work."

Having just painted almost every building on the ranch over the course of the past year, Hayley could say that she was no fan of painting, but she was good at it. Brush, roller, sprayer. She was a master of all. "Are you sure?"

"Positive. Besides, you probably shouldn't be exposed to paint fumes if you're going to try to get pregnant." Bella leaned forward before glancing first right, then left, as if making certain they were not overheard. "Any closer to a decision?"

The decision was not if, but when and how.

"Getting there, but I want to make certain I have all my ducks in a row."

Bella's gaze came up to look past Hayley, who shifted in her seat to see what had caught her friend's attention. A young woman in her early twenties, dressed in worn jeans, a western shirt with the sleeves rolled up to the elbows, and a battered felt hat with a feather in the band, approached. The light-brown braids she wore reached nearly to her waist.

"Excuse me . . . Hayley Parker?"

"Yes."

"I'm Andie Landry. I think you have my dog."

Bella's eyebrows rose as she met Hayley's gaze.

"I adopted a dog from the shelter," the woman continued. "And she got loose while I was at work and ran off."

"Where do you work?"

"I *worked* on the Hunt Ranch." Andie's expression tightened. "First my dog disappears, then they fire me. Not a good week, but I can take care of Greta. I'd feed her before feeding myself." She lifted her chin. "I just want her back."

"You got fired?"

Elena at Whiskers and Paw Pals had told her that the Hunt Ranch said she quit, but there was something about the girl's demeanor that made Hayley wonder which scenario was true.

"Yeah. They didn't like my attitude. I made the mistake of telling Mr. Hunt that he was using the wrong bit on his horse. Or at least I think that's why they fired me."

"You know bits?"

"I know horses," she said simply. "I thought I was hiring on as a day hand for the summer, handling horses and cattle, but I ended up doing housework in the lodge." Her tone bordered on disgust.

"Really."

"It was supposed to be a temporary thing, until they replaced their former housekeeper, and Mrs. Hunt was so nice about it, I agreed. But . . . I messed up." Her eyebrows went up. "Mr. Hunt did not appreciate getting horse advice from a housekeeper."

"Or any advice, I'm guessing," Bella said darkly. "My brother used to work for them." She lifted her cup, elbows planted on the table. "That said, Mrs. Hunt is nice, and Mr. Hunt contributes to many local causes, so"—she lifted her shoulders in a c'est la vie shrug—"his megalomania is, for the most part, overlooked."

"Not on my part." Andie spoke in a stony voice before turning to Hayley. "My grandparents live in Great Falls, and they'll take Greta until I get on my feet again."

Hayley studied the young woman, noted her short fingernails and work-roughened hands. "You're looking for a job." It was a statement, not a question.

Andie nodded. "I have a few leads." From the tone of her voice, they didn't sound like strong ones. "The important thing is that Greta will be taken care of until I land something. My grandparents have a fenced yard, and Greta loves their cat, so she'll be in good hands."

"I'll tell you what," Hayley said. "Can you meet me at Whiskers and Paw Pals to discuss Greta with Elena? She has to have the final say in what happens."

"When?"

"Say in an hour?" If she could get the Greta matter settled, she'd feel better. And if Andie needed a job, well, maybe they could help one another out in that regard.

Andie gave a solemn nod. "I'll be there."

TWO HOURS LATER, Hayley glanced in the rearview mirror at the big truck following her smaller one as she turned onto the Lone Tree Ranch Road. Interesting how a person could go to town to meet a friend for coffee and end up returning home with a temporary ranch hand, but that was how things worked out.

After an intense discussion with Elena at Whiskers and Paw Pals, who was all about the welfare of her charges, Greta was going back to Andie, and Andie was going to work on the Lone Tree. Hayley needed immediate help now that Vince was gone, and Andie needed a job until she could land something permanent. Permanent meaning "permanent with horses." Hayley, knowing how rare jobs in the equine field could be, silently wished her luck.

Andie parked next to her under the big elm tree that shaded the house. Greta jumped on the side yard gate, and Andie made a beeline for the little dog who started yipping and leaping at the sight of her mom. Any doubts Hayley had about Andie evaporated as the gate opened and Greta launched herself into Andie's arms. Uncontrolled wiggling and face kissing ensued, then a nudge on the back of her leg made Hayley start. Remy nudged her again, and Hayley reached down to rub the pig's bristly head.

"Thank you so much for finding her," Andie said, as she put the little dog on the ground. Almost immediately, she picked her back up again as the pig approached. "Aren't you a beauty?" she said to Remy, who grunted as she sniffed at Andie's shoes. Andie hugged Greta close. "And thanks for hiring me."

"I'll show you where you'll stay."

All Andie had with her were two duffel bags, her riding gear, and a plastic bag of pet supplies. She lifted one duffel out of the back of her truck and Hayley the other.

The duplex-style cottage that served as housing for seasonal employees had been built in the 1960s by Hayley's grandfather. Hayley had painted the building last summer as she buried herself in ranch repairs while dealing with the loss of her dad that spring. A small porch fronted the building, with two doors separated by a couple of feet of shiplap siding.

"Take your pick," Hayley said.

Andie gave a shrug. "The one on the left."

Hayley opened the door, and they went inside to drop the duffels on the floor near the small Formica table. They'd already established that Greta would stay in Hayley's yard while Andie was at work, and hashed out the details of pay and notice required before she moved on, but Andie seemed oddly distracted. Worried almost.

"Is everything all right?" Hayley finally asked before leaving her new hand to settle in.

Andie started to nod, then shifted her weight. "The thing that got me fired?"

"Telling Carter Hunt about his horse's bit?"

Andie nodded. "That happens to me a lot. Not the losing the job part, but pissing people off by blurting out the truth. I sometimes have a filter issue."

Hayley considered the woman's words. "Okay. You're saying I shouldn't ask you if these jeans make my butt look big?"

"It's not like I have no control. Ninety percent of the time, I stop and think before speaking. But that remaining ten percent can be deadly. And the bit Mr. Hunt was using on his horse was an abomination. It must have weighed a couple of pounds. Very showy. Probably a pricey antique, but that poor horse was way too young to be carrying that thing in his mouth."

"I might have said something, too, under those circumstances." Hayley hated it when people had no idea that they were causing an animal pain. Or worse, they knew, and didn't care. She decided to be charitable and put Carter Hunt in the first category. His wife did give generously to Whiskers and Paw Pals.

"I just wanted you to know that sometimes I say things I shouldn't."

"I appreciate it." She doubted that Andie would say anything that would grievously offend her, but one never knew.

Hayley said goodbye and left her new hand to settle in.

Tomorrow she'd pick up the water lease from Ken, then drive to the Keller Ranch to meet with Daniel Keller. She wondered if Spence would be there, since he'd been the one to put forth the issue, and she also considered the fact that she kind of wanted him to be there. Wanted to see him because . . . yeah. She was gratified that he'd stopped by the ranch during the windstorm.

Gratified and what else? There was more to this heady feeling she experienced while talking to the man.

Gratification and a sense of danger.

Interesting.

Hayley slowed her steps as she considered. What was threatening about Spence?

The way she reacted to him.

So it wasn't so much Spence as herself. Again, interesting.

She was realistic with herself regarding guys; what was possible, what was not. She hadn't seen many happily-everafters, and while she applauded those who managed to hold on to relationships through thick and thin, she hadn't experienced anything like that firsthand. Certainly, her parents hadn't set an example to follow.

Her dad never remarried after her mom left him, and it was now clear that Reba was looking for something she couldn't find. Being beautiful in an old-school, Rita Hayworth way and financially comfortable due to an inheritance, she had a lot of guys to choose from, but she inevitably chose wrong. Each new relationship was "the one." Then the cracks would appear, and eventually, the sledgehammer would come out, smashing the relationship to smithereens, then off Reba would go, looking for the guy who would give her a perfect life.

Fortunately, Hayley had gone to live with her father early enough in life to learn to be independent instead of guy dependent, and being a geek hadn't hurt in that regard. She'd watched her mom from the safety of the sidelines, hoping each new stepfather would be different, only to discover that they were basically all the same. And not one of them had the ability to connect with a child—aka her. Thankfully, she had limited time with them, but each and every one of them managed to make her feel like she had a third eye or something.

She put a hand on her flat abdomen and promised her future baby that she or he wouldn't have to deal with that shit.

Hayley went to bed early that night. Even though it was still daylight, she could see the warm glow of a light in the window of the left side of the duplex cabin. She nodded off almost immediately, jerking upright when the phone rang.

The house was dark, and she didn't bother checking the clock as she got out of bed and made her way to the kitchen where the landline phone sat on the desk where she did her accounts.

It rang again and, heart beating faster, because late-night calls were rarely good, she picked up the receiver and said hello.

Then she said hello again.

"Do yourself a favor and keep your water on your own property."

The line went dead.

A spark of anger ignited as Hayley set down the receiver. Really? Someone had called her late at night to warn her off?

Did . . . whoever . . . honestly think that a late-night call would sway her?

Maybe.

She was a woman alone on the ranch—or rather, she had been until bringing Andie home with her.

Who would know that she was thinking of leasing water?

She hadn't told anyone but Ken; however, she had no idea whom the Kellers might have told.

She walked across the dark kitchen to stare out the window. She could only see the duplex cottage by craning her neck, but the lights were off. She didn't even know why she was checking, other than idle curiosity and the need to distract herself while she got a grip.

The call was creepy, and she was reacting accordingly. Nothing wrong with that.

And it was probably going to be a while until she fell asleep again.

Whatever. She headed down the dark hallway and into her bedroom, which was partially illuminated by the outside porch light.

Nobody was going to scare her into doing their bidding. She might not seek out confrontation, might have spent a lot of her life making herself invisible to avoid it, but she'd changed over the past few years, and she wasn't taking this kind of crap lying down.

Tomorrow she was signing water lease papers right after she checked out Andie's tractor skills. Mr. Anonymous Caller could take a flying leap. No one was telling her what to do with her own property.

SPENCE WAS CHECKING the boundary fence along the county road before they turned their cattle into that pasture. It was open range, but cows on the road were a danger, especially at night, and the Kellers were careful about keeping their fences intact. He approached the junction between the county road and the long driveway leading to the ranch when a truck slowed and then turned down the drive.

He knew that truck. Now what he needed to know was if Hayley was there with good news or bad.

By the time he got back to the house, Hayley was seated at the kitchen table between Daniel and Audrey, going over the terms of the lease, which according to Daniel, were almost identical to the terms before, except for the price, which had gone up significantly.

Daniel looked up as he walked into the kitchen. "Good," he said simply. "I have something to discuss with you."

"Okay." Spence pulled out a chair and sat.

"Hayley here is having an issue."

"What's that?"

"I got a call warning me to keep my water on my own property."

Spence met his dad's gaze. "Really? Whoever could that be?"

"That's the question," Hayley said, drawing his attention. "As far as I know, no one knows that we discussed this matter."

"Unless Hunt simply put two and two together." Spence frowned at the table. "Although, he wasn't living here the last time we leased water from the Lone Tree." Carter Hunt had left his daughter on the ranch with a housekeeper while he traveled the world, nailing down his business deals, and had only recently taken up full residence on the ranch, which he now wanted to expand in a major way. Once an entrepreneur, always an entrepreneur.

"When did you get the call?"

"Last night. Just late enough to make it creepy. The voice was male, but I didn't recognize it. It sounded . . . younger than Carter Hunt."

"Are you leasing us the water?" Daniel asked in a patient voice.

"Of course. Even if I'd decided not to, the phone call would have changed my mind."

"It must have been Hunt." Spence could think of no one else with an interest in the matter.

"I can't see him doing anything that would blow back on him legally, but . . . if he could get away with some nefarious shit, I can see it," Reed said.

"If there's nefarious stuff happening," Audrey said, "then I worry about Hayley being alone on the ranch."

"I'm not alone," Hayley said. "I have a new hire staying with me." She hesitated before adding, "A person who worked for Carter Hunt until a few days ago." She shifted her attention to Spence. "She's the one who adopted the dog you found. We hooked up via the dog."

"This sounds kind of suspect to me," Reed said.

"A coincidence?" They happened, but Spence was always suspicious of things that fit together too precisely. Like this time frame.

"You found the dog before asking about the water lease,"

Hayley pointed out.

"When did this person get fired?"

"I don't know the timeline," Hayley said slowly. She regarded the table with a frown, then looked up. "I think she's legit."

"Even so . . ." Spence shifted, pulling his feet under his chair and propping his elbows on the table. "Maybe you need some day help."

"I totally need day help." Then she seemed to realize where he was going and abruptly added, "But not you."

Spence made a movement to indicate a stab to the heart. Hayley's cheeks went pink before she murmured, "It's not *you*. It's that I don't want to interfere with the reason you're back home. I'll squeak by until my high school kids are available. They show up early next week."

"Will this person from the Hunt Ranch be able to fill Vince's shoes?" Daniel asked.

"I'm assuming so."

Daniel leaned back in his chair, running his gaze over those gathered at the table. "Reed and I can handle matters here until . . . you know."

The surgery. Scheduled for the end of June, five weeks away.

"And Henry will probably still be here," Spence added before shifting in his chair. "Even if you don't need day help, you have a half-finished pipe corral, and you probably won't find a welder of my expertise who would finish it for the rate I charge."

She looked interested. "What rate is that?"

Spence shot a look at his dad, then said, "Half my going rate." He raised his eyebrows in a way that silently said, "After all, I owe you," and Hayley appeared to receive the message.

She sat back in her chair, her gaze traveling from one Keller face to the next until she hit Audrey, who gave a slight nod.

"We'd all feel better if you weren't so alone until we find out if this was just Carter Hunt taking a shot in the dark, or something else."

Hayley pulled in a long breath, then released it. "All right. How long do you think the corrals will take?"

"How about I work halftime at your place, halftime here until Dad's back operation? By that time, June . . . what?"

"Twenty-seventh," Audrey said automatically.

"By then we should know if anything else is going on, and if your new hire is a Hunt spy."

"Andie is not a Hunt spy." But despite the certainty of her words, Hayley didn't back away from the offer. "I'll pay you for the corrals and for any work you might do, just like I would anyone else who sets foot on the place."

"Agreed. Start tomorrow?"

Hayley looked as if she was still having a few second thoughts, but she said, "Yes. Tomorrow," before opening the folder sitting on the table in front of her. "Now that that's settled, let's go over what Ken drew up for us."

Chapter Five

UPON MEETING ANDIE Landry, Spence understood why Hayley didn't believe the young woman was an agent for Carter Hunt. All of maybe twenty-one or twenty-two, she had the look of a seasoned ranch hand, with nothing approaching artifice in her demeanor. She met his eyes directly and shook his hand when he introduced himself shortly after arriving on the Lone Tree Ranch.

"I don't know where Hayley is. She said something about the greenhouse."

"I'll find her," Spence said.

"You're the guy who found Greta?" she asked.

"I am."

"Thank you. I about died when she went missing."

"Glad it all worked out," Spence said with a half smile. He'd love to ask her about Carter Hunt, but decided against it. Andie wouldn't know if he'd called to warn off Hayley from leasing water.

Andie jerked her head toward the idling tractor. "I have ditches to mow along the driveway."

"Then I guess I'll find Hayley and get to work myself."

Hayley was in the greenhouse, just as Andie had said, watering flats that were just showing touches of green.

"Hey," she said. "Thanks for coming."

"Glad to. This gives my dad a chance to pretend that things aren't going to change at the end of June after his surgery."

"You're not here because you owe me?"

"I'm totally here because of that." But there was more to it than owing her. There was a sense that he needed to be here, and he went with it. Some of his most interesting life experiences had occurred because he'd followed instinct. His instinct now told him that Hayley, who was facing her first summer of farming and ranching without her dad or her foreman, needed help. She might not need his help specifically, but he was here, and thanks to Henry, had some time on his hands. He would do what he could, and if Carter Hunt called her again, he and Hunt would have a word. The man was noted for belligerence and intimidation tactics when he didn't get his way, and he hadn't gotten his way. Because of Hayley, he was going to have to have a bridge engineered across the rocky canyon that restricted access to the part of his property he wanted to develop. That probably wasn't sitting well.

"Did you meet Andie?" Hayley asked with a knowing smile.

"She is not a spy."

"I know, right?" Hayley's eyes crinkled in a fascinating

way as she gave him an I-told-you-so smile. "The Hunt Ranch's official story is that she quit, but she got fired for telling Carter Hunt that he was using the wrong bit on his horse."

"Then she can get unemployment."

"That she can. Unless they deny firing her."

"I wonder if they can get away with that?"

"Money talks," was all Hayley said.

"Amen to that." Spence tilted his head as he watched the sunlight that filtered through the frosted roof play off Hayley's red hair, bringing out glints of gold and burgundy.

"You're staring," she said.

"Sorry." He felt self-conscious, not exactly a familiar feeling for him, but one that seemed to occur regularly during his conversations with Hayley. "The sun makes your hair an amazing color."

"Having red hair can be like wearing an oversized purple hat. People comment."

Always one to take a hint, Spence stepped back. "I'll get my stuff ready, then let's talk about what and where with the corrals."

He could guess the layout with a decent degree of accuracy, but he didn't want to have to redo anything due to a miscommunication.

"I'll be there shortly."

She turned the hose back on and Spence made his exit, stopping at the door. He cleared his throat, then said, "My hair has gotten me into trouble too."

He caught the beginning of a smile before she turned the spray onto a young tomato plant.

"A story for another day," she said. "I have work to do."

AN HOUR LATER, Spence was picking through the pipe, determining quantities, since at least half of the pipe appeared to be salvaged, when a backfire in the distance brought his head up. A truck was approaching the ranch at a decent clip, and when the driver neared the cattle guard, he shifted down, causing another backfire, followed by the low-throated rumble of the manifold.

Spence had no idea where Hayley was—she'd disappeared after they'd discussed the corral and she'd given him the schematic her father had drawn on a yellow legal pad in black ink—but certainly she heard the approach of the Frankenstein truck with the straight pipes that were probably borderline illegal. The truck pulled to a stop and the engine abruptly died before two primer-gray doors opened. The kids—boys? men? They looked to be sixteen or seventeen—who got out of the truck were almost polar opposites. The driver was slightly built, with glasses and closely cropped blond hair. The passenger was taller, heavier, dark-haired, and looked like he dead-lifted cattle as a hobby.

"Hey," the driver said. "We're here to see Hayley."

"You're her summer crew," Spence guessed.

"Yep. Connor Johnson," the blond said. "And this is Ash Brown." He indicated his partner with a sideways jerk of his head.

"Spence Keller. I live next door." He rubbed a hand over the back of his neck as he searched for signs of life near the barn and greenhouse. Andie had brought the tractor in just before the boys drove up, so she and Hayley were there somewhere. "I'm sure she'll show soon." If she hadn't heard the truck, then she had something the matter with her ears.

"We don't start work until Monday," Connor said. "But Hayley likes to iron everything out before we start."

Sounded like Hayley. "You guys handle the irrigation and stuff?"

"We are intimately acquainted with hand line and wheel line," Ash said, referring to the more labor-intensive field irrigation systems. "We also swath, rake, bale, stack hay, move cattle, spray weeds."

"But we draw the line at fence repair." Connor gave Ash a look, then the two busted up laughing.

"We fix a lot of fence," Connor explained. "Last summer, Vince did the work of two guys in the fields so that we could do the work of four on the fences. Really bad winter damage."

"Hayley was shorthanded last year too?" Because she made it sound like this year was an exception.

"Not really. One of our friends was working with us last

summer and Vince always does the work of two guys because he can't help himself." Ash shifted his weight. "Hayley was still getting over her dad, and we all went the extra mile to help her keep busy, which is why the place looks like it does."

"All shiny and new," Connor added.

"It does look good," Spence said.

"This will be a more normal year. Ten-hour days instead of twelve or fourteen." Ash tucked a thumb into his front pocket as he stared out across the fields.

"Less pay, but also less painting," Connor added.

"Because there's nothing left to paint," Ash pointed out.

Spence nodded. "Yeah. I think you got it all."

"Are you going to be working here?" Ash asked.

"On and off," Spence said. "I'm building the pipe corrals and helping out where needed until my dad has back surgery. Then . . . I don't know."

"You won't be taking Vince's place?" Connor asked.

"That'd be Andie," Hayley said from behind Spence. He'd heard her footsteps as she walked behind the barn, but hadn't turned to see whether it was Andie or Hayley, because he knew without looking. "Spence is moving on after the summer is over, right?"

"I travel," he said to the boys.

"Traveling pays well?" Ash asked.

"It does when you're operating an arc welder."

"Ah." Connor gave him a thoughtful frown. "Do you get

paid . . . like . . . pretty well?"

"It's decent money," Spence said. "And I enjoy the traveling part. That said, not everyone is cut out for it."

"But you are?"

Spence shrugged. "Born under a wandering star."

The boys exchanged looks, as if unfamiliar with the saying, but neither Hayley nor Spence enlightened them.

Hayley gestured with her head toward the house. "Head inside and I'll find Andie, so that I can introduce you and line out what the summer's going to look like without Vince." She raised her eyebrows and said gravely, "No painting this year."

"Yay," Ash said half-heartedly before giving Hayley a genuine smile. "Looking forward to meeting this Andie person."

"I'm sure you are," Hayley said. "Just be careful she doesn't hurt your feelings."

"She?" Ash said at the same time that Connor said, "Our boss is a lady?"

"And she pulls no punches," Hayley added mildly.

"Punching boss," Ash said. "I like it."

"Punching *lady* boss," Connor said with a lift of his blond eyebrows.

"Careful or she'll have you for breakfast," Hayley called as the two started toward the house. Then she turned to Spence. "That's my crew."

"They seem competent."

"They're lovable smart-asses and totally dependable."

"Good." Spence shifted his weight. "I need to get going soon. Do you need help loading anything for the Farmer's Market?" The first of which was the next day. Hayley had already put up her canvas canopy, checked it for mildew and holes, then packed it away again.

"I have things under control. Andie is coming with me and"—she sucked in a breath and glanced over at her garden before looking back at him—"I've got this. It'll be fun."

"Good. I may see you there, since there's also a horse sale."

"Sounds good." Hayley cleared her throat.

"Right."

They stared each other down for another two or three seconds, then Spence turned and headed toward his truck, wondering why he suddenly felt like a junior high kid. It made no sense at all.

But it was kind of intriguing.

MARIETTA'S FIRST FARMER'S Market was held in conjunction with a stock horse sale at the fairgrounds. Because it was early in the season, the farm booths were, for the most part, scantily stocked with greenhouse produce, fresh-cut flowers, and seedlings ready to plant in home gardens. The artisan booths, however, were something to behold. Having had the winter months to produce inventory, the stock of wooden toys, blown glass, wrought iron, and leatherworks were something to behold, and the artisans were enjoying brisk sales.

With Andie's help, Hayley had set up early, then settled in to watch the other booths go up, occasionally helping with an uncooperative canopy or chatting with a friend. After setup, Andie got a horse sale catalog, then settled in the chair next to Hayley and perused the offerings with Greta curled up on her lap.

"That's a nice-looking animal," Hayley said, reading over Andie's shoulder.

"If only I had the money," Andie said with a sigh. She turned the page.

"Do you own a horse?" Hayley asked the obvious question that she'd never thought to ask.

"The horse I grew up with lives with my grandparents in Great Falls. All the colts that I'd bought and trained, I've sold." One corner of her mouth quirked up. "I got good money for them, but I'm holding off buying a horse until I have a place to keep it." She stroked Greta. "Which is where this one comes in. Not quite a horse, but great company and a better foot warmer at night."

Hayley had more questions about her temporary hire, but rather than pelt the girl with them all at once, she held off, figuring that they probably had the summer to get to know one another. In that regard, she was lucky because she'd received no hits on her help wanted posts. Everyone, it seemed, already had jobs nailed down for the summer. By fall, though, when some of those summer hires needed winter jobs, she'd have more luck. In the meantime, she had Connor, Ash, and Andie. And Spence, of course, but she didn't count him because once the pipe corrals were finished, his dad would have surgery, and he'd be back on his own ranch taking up slack.

She leaned back in her chair and closed her eyes for a moment, enjoying the feel of the late May breeze on her face. Her eyes opened at the sound of a familiar voice.

Spence. It was almost like she'd somehow conjured him up.

"Hey." Spence appeared in front of her booth with his brother Reed. "How's it going?"

"I've sold several six-packs. Plants, not beer," she said when Reed frowned. "But the big money is going to the woodworkers and jewelry makers. Those are the kinds of things out-of-towners buy. Most don't want to deal with seedlings."

"Understandable." Spence looked at Reed. "I think you need petunias in those window boxes of yours."

"Yes. Yes, I do," Reed said with a quick dark look at his brother, who grinned widely. He looked at the selection in front of him. "Any bright-pink ones? My daughter loves neon pink."

"These will be bright pink with white dots and splashes,"

Hayley said, pointing to a six-pack. "And these will be the same, only purple. I also have stripes and some kind of variegated ones."

Reed pulled his wallet out of his pocket. Hayley caught Spence's eye and her stomach did an odd little flip and drop as he winked. She put her hand on her abdomen where it was free-falling, then immediately put it back on the table.

The consequence of the thoughts you've been thinking about the man.

No doubt.

But . . . he didn't know about those thoughts, and she wasn't about to tip him off, so she met his gaze and gave him a confident smile. "Horse shopping?"

"Just browsing," Spence said.

"And socializing," Reed added. "Seeing Spence in the area is like spotting Bigfoot, and people are taking advantage."

As if to emphasize his point, an older man clapped Spence on the shoulder from behind. "Long time," he said.

"Coach Michaels." Spence shot Hayley a quick look, then stepped away with the retired coach. Hayley wondered if the man had any idea that she was responsible for the team winning the championship that year. Spence wasn't about to rat out the jerk who'd locked him in the equipment room, preferring to take care of matters in his own way. Someday she'd have to ask him just what that meant, and if he'd ever followed through.

"I'll grab some seats," Reed said to his brother after giving Hayley and Andie each a smiling nod. A few minutes later, Spence and Coach Michaels parted ways and Spence ambled back to Hayley's booth.

"That was a blast from the past," Spence said.

"Does he know?"

Spence shook his head. "I don't think Lucas ever let on to what he'd done, even long after the fact."

"Did you ever do anything about it?"

"Almost. Then I had second thoughts and decided to walk away. Knowing how things could get out of hand with Lucas, I left it as our little secret. Honestly? I think that made him more nervous than if I'd alerted the powers that be."

"Probably."

Spence glanced over his shoulder at the arena. "They'll be starting soon, and I want to take a look at a couple of horses."

Hayley nodded and then turned her attention to a customer. Andie returned to the booth and after the customer left with a bouquet of cut flowers, Hayley turned to her. "You should get a seat for the sale."

"Really?"

"I think I can handle the crowd," Hayley said dryly. Her offerings were meager compared to the non-produce booths.

"Then, yeah. I'll head in."

Andie pushed a long braid over her shoulder to join the

other and edged her way out of the booth. In the distance, Hayley caught sight of Spence once again being stopped by an old acquaintance.

She glanced down at her money apron. Was he really going to hit the road come fall, as he'd mentioned more than once?

She was fairly certain he was. He made no secret of wanting to continue his footloose existence and, as long as his family didn't need him, she felt certain he would do just that.

AFTER BEING STOPPED half a dozen times by old acquaintances who hadn't seen him in a while, Spence finally made his way to his seat next to Reed. After the third or fourth horse had sold, he started looking around. He wasn't horse hunting like his brother. He spotted Andie with her forearms leaning against the arena fence rails, watching the auction. Poor kid. Sucked in by Carter Hunt, then spit back out again.

In a way, he was glad, though, because it meant that Hayley wasn't alone on her ranch. Normally, that wouldn't bother him, or even be on his radar, but the call telling her not to lease water bothered him. He was going to be there during the day, building corrals, but the shit he was worried about went down at night.

That said, the water was flowing and as far as he knew, Hayley had received no more calls, so . . . yeah. It was a done deal, and Carter Hunt knew that. But one thing Spence knew about Hunt—he was a tenacious operator—which was why he was successful, and he would have another go at the Keller property in some way or another.

So was there a compromise? Spence couldn't think of one. And even if he could, he probably wouldn't entertain it. It wasn't his family's fault that Carter wanted easier access to the property he'd inherited from his brother than building a bridge across a deep canyon. Carter asked. They'd said no. That should have been the end of it.

He shifted his attention back to the arena, where a high-powered gelding was being ridden in by a five- or six-year-old kid. A bit of a ruckus caught his attention and he turned to see Andie in what looked to be a heated conversation with none other than Carter Hunt himself. He nudged Reed and pointed, then got to his feet.

"Want help?" Reed asked.

"No." The fact that Reed was engaged to the man's daughter made the situation a bit more complicated and Spence saw no reason to ruin Reed's day. Before he could edge his way down the crowded row of seats, Hayley appeared on the scene, taking a stance next to Andie, which only served to hurry his steps.

Spence was halfway to where Hayley and Andie were facing off with a red-faced Carter Hunt, when a kid Spence didn't know joined Andie and Hayley, apparently as an ally.

Spence slowed his steps, watching the foursome as he made his way toward them.

As he got closer, Spence heard Carter Hunt say, "This isn't a matter to be discussed in public."

Andie put her hands on her hips and jutted out her chin. "People need to know how you operate."

"Careful, young woman."

Andie lifted her chin and said in a loud voice, "If you fire someone, then try to convince the employment people that they quit, then people should know."

"You did quit."

"You fired me for telling you that you didn't know what you were doing." She turned to the people nearby, some of whom were openly gawking and others who were listening, but pretending not to. "This man was using a spade bit on a young horse who should have still been in a snaffle. Then he blamed the horse when it freaked out."

Carter Hunt was turning a nice shade of purple when a tall, neatly dressed cowboy, probably his manager, stepped in, but before he could commence managing, Carter turned on Hayley. "I don't know what your game is, but if you want to draw a line in the sand, remember that I am not someone you want to mess with."

Hayley's face went red with shock at the unprovoked attack. "Tell me about this line, because I have no idea what you're talking about." She took a step forward. "Do. Not.

Threaten. Me."

She enunciated each word, grinding them out from between her teeth. Spence stepped in behind her and Hunt's gaze rose to meet his over Hayley's head. Spence set his hands on her shoulders in a show of support. Her taut muscles became even tighter at the contact, then gave a little when he squeezed reassuringly.

"Mr. Hunt, they need you in the sales office," Carter's cowboy said. Hunt continued to stare down Hayley, who, despite her red cheeks, appeared patently unimpressed— "appeared" being the key word. He could almost feel the adrenaline pumping through her body.

She squared her shoulders, drilling Hunt with a look. "I leased water to the Keller Ranch, just as my dad did in the past, and I hired the person you fired. None of this had anything to do with you, because, despite what you believe, the world doesn't revolve around you."

"Let's go," Spence said, the words barely audible. But Hayley heard them. She glanced up at him, then back at Hunt.

Meanwhile, Andie looked like she was about to let fly, and as entertaining as that might be, Carter Hunt was a litigious man, and Spence deemed it best to get everyone out of there before something was said that qualified for a lawsuit.

"Come on," Hayley said to Andie. "My booth is unmanned."

Andie turned then, her eyes widening as she saw the guy standing behind her, as if at the ready. Then she nodded at Hayley and started toward the booth.

Hayley reached up to touch one of Spence's hands. "I'll talk to you later." He dropped his hands from her shoulders as she started toward her booth, leaving him standing beside the silent kid who'd come to back Andie, now facing off with Carter Hunt and his nervous-looking henchman.

"Leave her alone," he said to the man.

"Or?"

Spence smiled. "This is where I say something that you later have witnesses attest to, right?"

Hunt pulled in a long breath, fired a couple of death rays from his dark eyes, then shouldered his way past his manager and headed to the sales office. The manager glared at Spence, who gave an uncaring shrug, even though he was in the mood to throttle someone. He turned his attention to the kid who'd come to Andie's aid.

"Do I know you?" he asked curiously.

"Brandon Grady. I work for the Marvell Ranch."

"Ah." The Marvell Ranch was probably thirty miles away on the opposite side of the valley, but still part of the Marietta community.

"Andie and I had a college class together last year, but I don't think she recognized me."

Spence thought she did, but hadn't known how to handle the situation.

Brandon, who looked like he was twenty-four or -five, watched Hayley and Andie disappear into the crowd on their way back to the Farmer's Market, then turned back to Spence.

"I hate bullies."

"Then stay away from that guy," Spence said. "Buy you a beer?" He indicated the concession wagon with a lift of his chin, but the kid shook his head. "Thanks, but I have a horse to sell."

With that, he touched the brim of his black felt hat, and headed toward the temporary pens where the horses awaited their turn in the arena.

HAYLEY PULLED IN a calming breath, then exhaled, causing Andie to give her a curious look.

"I don't like confrontation," she said. "It makes me feel like I'm going to jump out of my skin after it's over and I have time to think."

"Then keep deep breathing, but don't pass out on me," Andie said. She shot a quick look over her shoulder toward the spot they'd just left. Hayley did the same, glad to see that Carter Hunt had gone on his important way.

"I'm not going to pass out. I might not like confrontation, but I don't avoid it." Not in most cases, anyway. "Some battles need to be fought."

Andie help up a palm, which Hayley touched with her own. "Amen."

"How'd that all start, anyway?"

"He received the notification that I applied for unemployment benefits. There were no witnesses to my firing, so he can contest it." Andie ducked under the rear of the canopy and took a seat while Hayley rearranged her seedlings to fill in the spots left from purchases. "He just wanted me to know that it would be easier if I let the matter slide. No hearing and all that. Like I mind telling my side to a judge."

"As if," Hayley agreed. She couldn't see Andie being hesitant to explain anything to anyone. She was envious. Yes, she had come out of her shell, but she always felt as if she were only one cutting comment away from disappearing back inside again.

But you aren't.

"Nice of Spence to back us up," Andie observed, and before Hayley could agree, she added, "Do you know the other guy? The quiet one?"

"I kind of recognized him from some local events, but I don't know anything about him."

"I think we had a class together at Montana State. Big lecture hall thing, but yeah. I think he was there." She gave Hayley a sideways look. "Kind of invisibly there."

"I know what that's like."

"I'm not surprised."

Hayley gave a short laugh as she took her seat beside Andie, who in turn gave Hayley a look. "Too blunt?"

Hayley shook her head before smiling at a pair of women who stopped to look at the broccoli and cauliflower starts.

After the ladies paid for their purchases and headed back to their cars with the plants, Andie said, "All I meant was that you're nice. Diplomatic. I can see where you might keep quiet and see how things played out before intervening. But I loved the way you fired up when Mr. Hunt got in your face." She wrinkled her nose. "Nice work."

"Thank you. And yes, I try for diplomacy, but I'm not letting people walk on me. I didn't do it back when I was too shy to talk to people, and I won't now."

"You were too shy to talk to people?" Andie ran a hand down one long braid.

"Thus, the invisible years."

"Huh." Andie looked as if she had no idea what it would be like to be invisible. "Did you find that the red hair kind of worked against you?"

Hayley laughed and pushed said red hair over her shoulders with both hands. "Redheads are supposed to be quiet geeks or raucous rebels. I was the geek variety. Braids. Glasses. All I was missing was the tin grin—not that people saw my teeth, because I rarely spoke."

"What changed?"

"Long story," Hayley said, stretching her legs out in front of her. The crowd had thinned as the horse sale progressed, and she had a feeling that the big rush was over. She could relax.

"I have time," Andie said, before biting her lip. "Unless that's too pushy."

Hayley generally didn't tell her story, because . . . who cared? But Andie continued to regard her with open curiosity, so Hayley said, "My mom is kind of a serial bride. She marries . . . I don't know why she marries, but I had four stepdads before I reached eighteen. That's why I chose to live with my real dad on the Lone Tree when I was eleven. I could just be me." She inhaled, watching a mother kneel down to replace a shoe her toddler had walked out of. "But I had a hard time being me in public, so I got some counseling when I started college, and lucked out and got someone I could work with and confronted my issues."

When she glanced over at Andie, the girl was staring at her with open admiration. "Good for you. I have a cousin who's shy, and I think he's still in his parents' basement. He's thirty-five."

Hayley gave a soft laugh. "I could do all this stuff on the ranch, which told me I was competent and confident in the right environment. I wanted to live all of my life that way. So I started doing things that made me uncomfortable and lived to tell the tale."

"How about him?" Andie said, lifting her chin. Hayley looked up to see Spence approaching the booth.

Hayley's heart gave a guilty jump. "What about him?" she asked, startled at the sudden change in topic—or maybe startled by the appearance of the topic himself.

"I think he likes you."

Another heart jolt as she recalled the comforting feel of his hands on her shoulders and that gentle squeeze saying that he had her back. It might be because they were facing a joint adversary or . . . he might like her. She could deal with him liking her, knowing that he was likely to take off to who knew where at a moment's notice.

"He owes me. Or he did. We're even now." Hayley shot Andie a quick look and abandoned diplomacy. "No big deal, but nothing I want to talk about."

Andie gave a matter-of-fact nod, seemingly fine with being told the subject was off-limits.

Bluntness had its upside.

Chapter Six

SPENCE IGNORED HIS phone as he laid out the chalk line for the corrals. He had a good idea who it was, and sure enough, when he took a break and fished his phone out of the jacket lying on the tailgate of his truck, Millie's name was on the screen. Missed call. Missed call. Missed call.

Spence hit her name and, a few seconds later, she answered. "Finally," she said, instead of hello.

"What's up?"

"I have a job. A quick one."

"My dad's surgery is in a few weeks."

"You'll be back by then. I have a guy out and need a replacement, pronto."

Spence shifted his jaw sideways. With the exception of working on Hayley's corrals, and keeping an eye on her place in case Hunt did anything stupid, which no one expected him to do now that the water was flowing on the Keller Ranch, he was at loose ends until after the surgery. He was supposed to take Henry's place when he returned to the ranch, allowing the old man to retire, but Henry wasn't easing toward the door, and frankly, with both he and Henry in one job, there wasn't enough to do. And, in Millie's defense, he usually went where she needed him. That said, they'd had a discussion in which she'd promised to only call if she were desperate.

Or thought she was desperate. Since Millie was a touch reactionary, so it was hard to tell which it was.

With the exception of Hayley's corrals, which he'd finish before leaving in October, he was in a good place to take the short contract . . . but he didn't want to.

When had that ever happened before?

He'd had contracts that he knew going in would be pains in the butt, but he took them. And completed them efficiently and on time, just as he should take this contract and finish it efficiently and on time, then return to the ranch to help Reed and Henry as the hay harvest got underway.

He had a sneaking suspicion that the reason he didn't want to take this contract was because of Hayley and some misguided protective instinct.

Her crew was young, but seemed to know what they were doing, and other than one desperate phone call from Hunt (probably), there'd been no repercussions to her leasing water to his family. What could Hunt do about that now?

Spence was certain that the man would channel his energy into other venues, so . . .

"I'll let you know tomorrow."

"Not a second later," Millie said.

"Check with Dawson. He might be the man for the job."

Millie let out a sigh. Dawson was an excellent welder, but something of a loose cannon. If he made it to the jobsite, then all was well. It was getting him there that was the problem. "Don't wish that on me."

When he ended the call, he turned to see Hayley standing a few yards behind him.

"Yes, this is me. Eavesdropping," she said as she casually leaned a shoulder against the heavy bay door beam.

He pushed his hat back, grappling again with the change in the woman. Confidence was sexy and, in Hayley's case, also intriguing. He'd gotten a glimpse of the steel beneath her shy exterior years ago, but after the incident, she'd gone back to keeping her gaze down as she negotiated the hallways of the high school and walking as if she didn't want to be noticed. Come to find out, she had, and he'd fallen down on the job. But he'd been eighteen and pretty focused on himself, so he gave himself a pass for that. It was the present that interested him.

The woman standing near the door did not have her gaze down. She seemed to be assessing him. No. She was definitely assessing him. He met her gaze with a quizzical look, and her cheeks went red.

"Sorry," she said. "I was just thinking what a difference ten years makes."

"You're saying I've changed?"

She gave him a surprisingly sassy smile. "You still have

the same devil-may-care attitude."

"But . . ."

She gave an innocent shrug. "But nothing."

"Uh-huh."

She continued to hold his gaze, but the color in her cheeks had deepened, and he took a swaggering step forward. "What's changed, Hayley?"

She tilted her head, pretended to consider, and he wondered if her heart rate had amped up as they faced off as his had.

"I'm having a hard time reconciling this you with the lanky kid I drove to the basketball finals." He lifted an eyebrow and she said simply, "You've filled out."

Spence made his mouth a hard line to keep from laughing, but he flexed an arm. "I've been working on my guns."

"Me too."

"Let's see."

Hayley gamely rolled up her sleeve and flexed. Yes, she had been working on her guns, or daily life on the ranch had done it for her.

"It didn't sound like you want to take the job."

"Yeah. But I should. It's short and I'd be back before the surgery. Unless things go sideways."

"So you're not taking it in case things go sideways?"

"I want to be here when the folks need me. Henry was supposed to retire a few months ago, but he isn't. He just keeps working, and even my dad, the guy who bulldozes his way through any situation, hasn't had a sit-down with him. They just keep paying his monthly salary, and he just keeps earning it."

"Huh."

"So I have no reason not to take a short contract." Now he was talking more to himself than to her. Saying it out loud didn't change the fact that it felt wrong, and Spence was a guy who followed his gut.

"Once Dad's back on his feet, I'll have plenty of contracts."

"Why no roots, Spence?"

He gave her a look. "Sometimes I wonder that myself." He had no answer other than he didn't like being tied down. Never had.

"There's a reason."

"Yeah?" he asked on a softly challenging note. "Any guesses as to what that might be?"

"Middle child between the wild older brother and the adorable twins. I think you grew up going your own way and have no reason to live any other way."

"Is that a note of approval I hear?"

"I think"—she said slowly—"that you're being true to yourself."

"I guess I am." And he'd never thought about his independent streak having something to do with his birth order, but it probably did. He'd discovered the benefit of being the odd man out decades ago. While the folks were focused on whatever Reed was up to, while simultaneously being exhausted by the workload of young twins with vivid imaginations, he'd been left to his own devices. And loved it.

But it also might have made him a touch self-centered. He did what he wanted when he wanted. And he had to say that he was a smoother operator than Reed. When he and his friends had embarked on adventures that may have landed them in deep trouble, they made contingency plans. Reed had not.

"How about you?"

"What about me?"

"You've changed."

"I have. Worked hard at it too." She pushed off the doorframe. "If you take this job, the corrals will still be here when you get back. They've been nothing but a pile of pipe for nearly four years, so a few weeks won't change anything."

"Noted."

"I'm serious, Spence."

"So am I."

She gave him a look that clearly said she knew something else was going on, and that she'd like to know what. He'd be happy to tell her if he knew.

"Take the job, Spence. I appreciate all your help, but it can wait."

"I might not have the time after Dad's surgery."

"A chance I'll take."

"Are you kicking me off the Lone Tree?"

She considered. "Is that what it'll take?"

"Did it ever occur to you that I may not want to take the job?"

"Is that true?"

Yes, but since he didn't know why exactly, he merely shrugged. Hayley wasn't having it. "Sidestepping, Keller?"

There was something about her challenging tone that had him narrowing his eyes. "You got a problem with that?" he growled, and Hayley laughed, a wonderful throaty laugh that made him want to make her laugh again.

"I think you should take the job."

"I think you've never welded in the southwest in the early summer."

"Probably better than in the dead of summer."

"You have a point." He indicated the lines he'd marked. "A good rain will take them away."

"We'll do them again."

"We?"

Now she shrugged. "Why not?"

He smiled a little, enjoying the way the sunlight turned her hair aflame, but knowing better than to stare after the last time she'd called him out for commenting on her hair. "I'll think about it. In the meantime, I'll do this."

"Good enough. Just one more thing." She ambled a few steps closer, until the toes of their blunt-toed leather boots were only a few inches away from one another. "You're not hanging around because of that late-night phone call, are you?"

One corner of his mouth tightened. "A little bit."

"I'm good. He's not going to do anything now that the water is flowing."

Spence put a hand on the back of his neck and squeezed the taut muscles there as he looked down at Hayley. Her features were delicate, but there was no denying the strength in her expression. Whoever had helped her come out of her shell had done a good job.

Or maybe it had been all her.

The air between them went oddly still as they regarded one another. Spence felt as if he couldn't—or maybe it was shouldn't—move and thus break the spell. The moment stretched and hit the point of near awkwardness. Something was going to happen. It felt inevitable and who was Spence to defy fate?

The afternoon light slanted over them, turning Hayley's hair to fire and warming Spence's back. He reached out to lightly trace the back of his finger down the side of her face.

Her lips parted at the contract, but she didn't back away.

It was odd how one night of shared adventure years ago made him feel like he knew her. Maybe he did, on a primal level. Maybe that shared experience had cut to the essence of their beings. And maybe that was why she was looking at him in a way that caused his groin to stir.

Oh, yeah. Just what he needed. He shouldn't have touched her.

But he did, and now he was about to touch her again. He leaned in as her hands came up the front of his jacket to lightly touch his face, then brought his head down until their lips met, drew apart, then met again. Spence realized several seconds in that he could lose himself in this woman in a serious way. There were things about her that he wanted to know. Things that he wanted to discover. But, for the moment, he contented himself with exploring her mouth as he pulled her close.

When their lips finally parted, Hayley dropped her gaze and eased back a step, her hands falling away from his upper arms. It was the first time he'd seen her revert to her old self, but almost as quickly as her gaze went down, it came back up again.

"I shouldn't have done that," she said, her eyes wide as she regarded him. He hoped they weren't wide with horror.

"It was kind of a joint effort."

A short laugh escaped her lips. "I don't want to send the wrong vibe, that's all."

"What vibe is that, Hayley?"

Her color started rising, but her expression was business-like when she said, "The vibe where I'm looking for . . ." She gestured. Spence didn't guess at what she meant because he wanted to know exactly where they stood.

"I'm all about sailing my ship alone," she finally replied after the silence had stretched to the point of being uncomfortable.

"If you're telling me not to read too much into things, I get it."

"You do?"

"I'm not looking for anything either."

The look of relief on her face might have been ego-denting, if she hadn't kissed him so enthusiastically a few minutes ago.

Her smile was just crooked enough to convey both gratitude and a touch of rueful honesty. "I have to tell you that I haven't partaken in too many casual kisses, so maybe I panicked?"

"Exactly the response I intend when I kiss someone."

The smile became more genuine at the wry comment, then she let out a breath that made her shoulders drop. "I guess I didn't need to say anything."

"About what?"

"Not looking for anything. A guy who spends as much time on the road as you do . . . well, you've probably made a choice not to get tied down."

He hadn't made that choice, but he did not correct her, because she was right in a way. He loved his life right now, traveling, being his own boss. But was he going to love it forever, as in never put down roots? When he thought of his distant future, he kind of visualized himself settled somewhere. But that was fodder for a long think on another day.

"Then I guess we understand each other. No worries." And probably no more kissing, because he could still feel the soft pressure of her lips and the way his body stirred as her tongue had gently teased his.

"I have something on the stove." She gave him a wry look, obviously thinking he thought she was making an excuse to escape. "I honestly do."

"Then you better go check on it."

"Right." She turned and headed into the barn and a moment later he heard the door at the front of the building open and shut.

All righty then. Spence rubbed his hand over the back of his neck again and regarded the pipe. Maybe it would be best if he took the job Millie was offering. He'd never been one to run away from a situation and this thing with Hayley was starting to feel like a situation.

It also felt different that anything he'd experienced before and maybe some time away would allow him to get his head on straight. And maybe Henry would stop coming to work by the time he got back?

Time would tell.

YOU NEED TO kiss Spence Keller more often.

The thought cartwheeled through Hayley's head time and again as she went about her business that day, along with snippets of the conversation that had followed. She loved how he'd simply accepted that she was happy with her life as it was, probably assuming that she and he were similar in that regard.

Were they?

Maybe, but she didn't think it was for the same reasons. She had a pretty clear vison as to why Spence was a rolling stone—she might be off base, but she didn't think so—and it wasn't the same as the reason she wasn't looking for a partner in her life. Even if their reasons were different, the result was the same, and the knowledge that they were on the same page in that regard had a crazy thought pushing its way into her head.

Crazy, yet . . . not.

It would solve a lot of problems . . .

Or cause more.

Hayley did not back away from the debate—if anything, she embraced it. *What if, what if, what if?*

"Hayley?"

She looked up to see Andie's head poke through the doorway. "Yeah?"

"You've got some serious fence issues in the north pasture. A tree came down and wiped out a good section. It's going to take chainsaws and manpower."

Hayley was glad that she wasn't putting any animals in that pasture for the next six weeks. She wiped her palms down her pants. "It must have come down in that windstorm we had a couple weeks ago."

Andie nodded, then said, "What do you want to do

about it?"

"I'll ride out and take a look, let you know."

"Great." She nodded, then said, "Are you okay with me taking off after work?"

"Why wouldn't I be?"

"I just wanted to make sure. The Hunts were more about the staff not leaving until their official days off. We were 'on call,' which usually meant cleaning up some mess."

"On this ranch, you're free as soon as you're off the clock. Big plans?"

"You remember that guy we met at the horse sale? Brandon Grady."

"The one you thought you had class with?"

"Yes. That one. He called me and asked if I wanted to have a drink, and . . . I do." She smiled.

"How did he get your number?"

Andie glanced down. "I have ads up at the feedstore and Big Z's, offering to start and train colts. I put them up the day you hired me and never took them down. I'll take them down when I meet Brandon."

"Or leave them up. If you want to train in your spare time, I'm okay with that."

"No offense," Andie said, "but I don't see having a lot of spare time."

She was right. They had tons to do, and what had she done? She'd encouraged a guy that could help them out to take another job.

"You have a point, but maybe in the fall?"

"Maybe."

Hayley pressed her lips together as she followed Andie out of the barn. Fencing issues were normal, especially after a stormy winter, but she would have appreciated not having a major repair facing her down when she was shorthanded. She'd told Spence that she and Andie and her high school crew could handle matters—and they could—but they didn't need extra work on top of the seasonal chores.

Andie headed to her bunk and Hayley to the greenhouse to check the temperature there.

Spence would be back, and she imagined that unless things got crazy on the Keller Ranch, he'd lend a hand where needed. She appreciated that, and she wondered if they'd cozy up to one another again.

Probably not. Cozying would muddy waters that she wanted to be crystal clear—if she was brave enough to follow through with her crazy idea.

Time, it seemed, would tell just how brave she was able to be.

SPENCE TOOK THE contract. It was either that or block Millie's calls. But he made it clear that this was the last contract until fall. He and Henry and Daniel had a heart-to-heart prior to him accepting the job, during which time

Spence realized just how frightened the older man was of the huge life change. What would he do with his time, having no family to speak of?

"You'll stay here on the ranch," Daniel said. "But Henry, no offense, you're slowing down."

The old man let out a sigh. "I know. But I can't stay if I don't earn my keep."

"You've already done that. If you don't stay in your trailer, the mice will move in."

The old man cocked an eyebrow.

"You're family, Henry. Stay in the trailer. Work when we need an extra pair of hands, but for Pete's sake, set a retirement date."

"End of the month."

Daniel cocked an eyebrow at Spence. "Does that work for you?"

"I can take that contract Millie's been hounding me about."

"Can I still work?" Henry asked. "I mean after I retire. Like let's say you need someone to swath a field."

"Only after you take off three months. Then, if you want to work, we'll discuss."

"Three months?"

Spence nodded at his dad. "That works for me. After this contract, I'll make certain Millie understands that I'm unavailable until the end of September."

"Cade's coming back during his hiatus, and who knows,

maybe he'll stay." Daniel gave Henry the eye. "Because this one won't."

"I'll be back on the road come October," Spence affirmed to Henry. "This is Mom's best shot at getting another kid closer to home." He gave his dad a look. "I do visit frequently."

"And we appreciate that, son."

Once the Henry retirement business was seemingly settled—seemingly, because Spence wasn't convinced that Henry was going to quit voluntarily when the time came—Spence called Millie, who in turn let out a grateful *woot*.

"Last time until October."

"I promise."

"I'm blocking your number until then."

"Spence . . . fine. Block me. Just take this contract."

So he did, leaving early Sunday morning to drive to southern Nevada, with plans to return eight days later—unless something went sideways. As it always did.

ANDIE LANDRY WAS a woman who put her head down and worked at a task until it was not only done, but done well. Carter Hunt's loss was Hayley's gain, which was why Hayley came to a dead stop outside the barn she'd been about to enter when she heard Andie say, "I appreciate the offer, but I made a commitment."

Andie had an offer? And judging from the regret in her voice, it was one she would like to take. Hayley walked through the barn door. Andie's head came up. She said a quick goodbye, then pocketed her phone.

"Ready to go," she said, hoisting the saddle next to her.

"Great. Uh . . . I overheard your conversation." Which was kind of becoming a habit with her. First Spence, now Andie. "Do you have a job offer?"

Andie's cheeks went rosy, a response that was probably not all that common for the woman. "That was Brandon Grady's boss on the Marvell Ranch. Their horse trainer is pregnant and just got ordered to scale back because she's expecting twins. They're looking for someone."

"And he called you."

Andie nodded. "Brandon recommended me. But don't worry. You need me, and I'm not going anywhere."

Hayley considered this as she went into the tack area and collected her own saddle. "Maybe you should."

"Excuse me?"

This was not a wise business decision, but Hayley couldn't help herself. "You signed onto the Hunt Ranch to work with horses, and they put you in a housekeeping position. Here you're a jack of all trades. I think that if this job involves horse training, you should take it."

It was obvious from Andie's expression how badly she wanted to. "I made a commitment."

"Andie . . . I can get someone else."

Andie studied her, obviously torn. "Liar."

"No. Really. I have the names of some guys who can help temporarily until Spence gets back."

"Spence is coming back?"

"Yes." She spoke as if she was surprised that Andie didn't know. "Call back. Tell them you talked to your employer, and she understands."

"Really?" Andie asked softly.

"Yes. For heaven's sake, how many horse training jobs are out there?"

"Not that many."

"Exactly. If you can do what you love full time, then do. I really appreciate the fact that you were going to let it go because I hired you, but . . . don't. This is a rare opportunity."

"It really is."

"You and Greta will have a great time on the Marvell Ranch. And who knows, maybe it'll lead to something full time."

As could her job here on the Lone Tree, but taking care of fences and cattle was not where Andie's love lay.

"Are you sure?"

"I am." She was sure that Andie should take the job and equally sure that she was setting herself up for some hardship, but she had to do the right thing. "If things don't work out, you can have this job back."

"That's really generous." Andie looked like she was going

to hug herself, and Hayley suspected that she was trying not to smile too broadly.

"Make the call, then we'll ride out to see that fence damage."

"I will. And . . . thank you!"

"No problem."

She hoped.

THE WIND WAS rising, and dark, blueish-gray clouds welled over the mountains when Hayley emerged from her greenhouse, feeling frazzled. Tomorrow would be busy, as would the following day and the day after that. Connor and Ash were good at what they did, but without Andie, who'd been on the Marvell Ranch for over a week, the day-to-day of the ranch was going to fill her hours until she hired someone else. She'd never had manpower problems before.

You never crossed Carter Hunt before.

But honestly, as much as she loved a good conspiracy theory, she didn't think he was responsible for the missed interview that day. It was harder to find day labor, and until now, she'd been fortunate. The people her dad had hired came back year after year, but this particular crew was aging out. The high school boys would soon be college boys, and after completing their freshman year at U of M, Hayley didn't think they'd return.

Get through this summer and worry about that later.

Right. But in the meantime, she had cattle to move on Saturday, and the next time she moved them, it would be to the pasture where the tree had destroyed the fence. She hoped that Spence would help her, but there was a good chance that he wouldn't return to her ranch after she put her plan into action and dropped her bombshell.

Should she wait to drop it until after the fence was fixed?

That was manipulative, and she wouldn't go there. She was going to be straightforward and honest. And she would look him in the eye while she was doing it.

In the meantime, she wouldn't be able to partake in the Farmer's Market that week due to moving the cattle. She was allowed two no-shows per summer, with notice, so that the organizers could find a fill-in before she lost her spot and had to start the application process again.

If she got dumped, she'd roll with it. The ranch was her livelihood. The greenhouses and gardens were her side gig. And when she had her baby, she'd have to cut back her work schedule, and there was a good chance that she wouldn't be indulging in gardening and such for a while. Time would tell on that matter, but the ranch supported her and got first priority.

Hayley ducked her head against the wind and headed to the barn. The hoes needed sharpening, and there was no time like the blustery present. She had just opened the main door when she heard an engine over the wind. Her heart jumped at the sight of Spence's truck.

You're not ready. Not even remotely ready.

But she didn't need to tackle the matter just yet. She didn't even need to do it today. She could make an appointment with him so that they could discuss the matter in a neutral environment.

She stood in the open doorway as Spence pulled to a stop, holding onto her hair to keep it from blowing around her face. He jumped out of his truck and headed toward her, following her into the barn, then shutting the door after himself.

"Some weather."

"Probably different than where you were."

"Nope. Thunderstorms every night."

"How was the job?"

"Hot. Short. Lucrative."

"Are you glad you took it?"

"It helped Millie get out of a bind, so yes. It kind of flummoxed her when I decided to come home for the summer."

"You don't actually work for them? I mean—"

"I'm a subcontractor. In theory, which allows me to pick my jobs. In reality, I never turn them down."

"You like all the travel?"

She sounded like she was trying to reassure herself on the point, and Spence picked up on it, shooting her a frown as he said, "Freedom is good. I get edgy when I feel tied down."

Hayley stayed silent, having learned during her invisible years that people often talk more, and she could therefore talk less, if they have time to think things through. She was about to conclude that Spence had nothing more to say when he gave a soft laugh.

"I guess it makes no sense, really. I had a great childhood. Parents were supportive. If they'd known everything I'd been up to, they might have had some things to say, but as long as the evidence didn't hit them in the face, they let me go my own way."

"I think Reed kept them on their toes."

"And Em. Yes." Spence rubbed his hands over the planes of his cheeks. "I don't know, Hayley. I think your birth-order theory has merit, so I'll go with it. Middle child syndrome."

"Do you have a girlfriend?"

He gave her a startled look, making Hayley wish she'd eased into the matter more smoothly.

"Had one."

"That was a personal question. Sorry." It was also a question she needed an answer to. Not that a girlfriend would necessarily be a problem, but it would add another facet to a tricky situation.

"This isn't a job interview, is it?"

She didn't answer, and he gave her a questioning look. There was no easy way to approach this matter. She'd thought about scheduling an actual appointment with him in a neutral, yet private, location. This wasn't an appointment, but they were alone in the barn, so . . .

She pushed back her hair. "Do you remember that pamphlet on my kitchen table the first time you came to my place?"

"I noticed the title."

"I plan to have a baby."

The silence that followed made Hayley shift her weight awkwardly as she watched Spence digest her bald statement.

"Alone?" he finally said.

"Yes." She lifted her chin, refusing to give her inner shyness the upper hand.

"That's a huge undertaking. I mean, alone and all."

"Lots of people do it. Women and men. I have my reasons and I have the resources to raise a child."

And didn't she sound defensive? She cleared her throat and focused on the fingers she'd been twisting together until she realized what she was doing. She carefully placed her hands on her thighs, spreading the fingers in an effort to relax them. "I know what I want, Spence."

"I think you'll be a great mom."

"Thank you." Hayley's gaze jerked sideways at the sound of something hitting the barn. They exchanged a look, then went to the door. Huge hailstones clattered to the ground.

"I'll open the bay door," she said. "Get your truck inside."

She didn't have to say it twice. Spence darted outside,

wincing as the hailstones pelted him. He jumped into his rig, had it in gear almost as soon as the engine turned over, and drove it into the barn. Hayley swung the door closed as he turned off the engine, then got out to check for damage.

There were some small dents and dimples in the hood, but in Hayley's opinion, nothing he couldn't knock out. He was lucky, judging from the sounds of the hail pounding on the roof, not to have lost a windshield. She was very thankful that she always parked her truck under a roof and hoped the tractors would be okay.

He turned to face her. "So, where were we?"

"I was about to ask if you would consider being the father of my child."

The words sounded starker stated aloud than they had in her head, and Spence looked like he'd been struck by a freeze ray.

"In a medical way," she blurted. He continued to stare at her as if she'd grown horns. "I'm not looking for anything other than . . ." Her voice trailed.

"Sperm?"

She lifted her chin, wondering how she'd lost control so quickly. Perhaps because of the subject matter. "I want to know the donor, but . . . that's it. There'd be no—"

"Yeah. I get it." He glanced down, as if trying to regain equilibrium. "That's a helluva ask, Hayley."

She felt her cheeks light on fire, but he continued before she could form a reply, raising those cool blue eyes and locking on her gaze before saying, "We would enter into a . . . partnership?"

She cleared her throat and her voice sounded remarkably normal as she said, "It would be a partnership until I get pregnant."

"Then . . ."

"That's it. I take it from there."

"I wouldn't be involved in the pregnancy, or share custody or anything?"

"I'd like my child to know who their father is. That's the point of a known donor. Medical history, like that. Also, kids wonder, and I want to have an answer, but I would have sole custody."

"But I'd have a kid."

Hayley sensed the *no* coming hard and fast, and felt the need to backtrack before it struck. In other words, she began to panic, something she'd promised herself she would not do.

"Maybe this wasn't such a good idea, Spence."

He tilted his head as he regarded her. "You caught me off guard. I mean . . . short of a marriage proposal—"

"I get it," Hayley said. She got to her feet and clapped her hands together. "Moving on."

"I'm not sure I can," he muttered.

This was going even worse than she'd anticipated in her worst-case scenario contemplations, and she needed to end it. Now.

"Spence, thanks for checking on me. I'm good." Total lie, but if it got her out of this awkward situation, then she was going with it. "Sorry to hit you with the sperm donor thing. I thought, what with your vagabond ways . . ." She made a gesture.

"I get it. I just can't see fathering a child, then moving on."

"And that's one of my criteria, so"—she forced a smile—"not a match."

Spence blew out a breath, then gave her a sidelong look, as if he could get the answers to the questions beating around in his head by reading her mind.

"Why single motherhood?"

Now she let out a breath. "I'm not partner material."

"How so?"

"Do you know my mom?"

"By reputation only."

"Need I say more?"

"Maybe you take after your father?"

"Who married my mother?"

"Point taken."

"I'm twenty-eight years old. There's a history of fertility issues in the family and according to my doctor, I'm looking at a ticking clock. I want children. I've thought this out, Spence."

He lifted his palms as if warding off criticism. "I'm sure you have, Hayley. You're a thinker."

"Thank you?"

"It was a compliment," he affirmed before lowering his gaze to his boots.

"The old me wants to apologize for asking. The new me says to take the hit and move on. I appreciate all the help you've given me, Spence."

He met her gaze in a serious way. "You still need help on the ranch. I heard that Andie has a new job." She didn't answer and he said, "I may not be on board for . . . donating . . . but I'm your friend, and I won't leave you high and dry."

Your friend.

In spite of being on fire with embarrassment, the words touched her. She wondered if they were true.

"What about your ranch?"

"Henry's working until the end of the month. I'll be done by then."

"You'd make more money taking welding contracts."

"But I wouldn't be close to home in case I am needed." He settled his hands on Hayley's shoulders.

"So, no to baby daddy. Yes, to ranch work." No easy task to speak as if she wasn't mortified, but all things considered, she was holding her own. Of course, she'd melt into a puddle of humiliation after Spence left.

"That sums it up." He started to lift his hand, hesitated, then touched her, tipping up her chin with his thumb and forefinger so that their gazes met and held even after he dropped his hand. "I can't have a child in this world that I have no say about."

"I get it." She did. She'd feel the exact same way. Why had she thought that Spence would feel differently? "I guess the very qualities that made you my number one choice also take you out of the running."

"I'm honored to be your number one choice."

She smiled gamely. "Can you go now?"

He smiled back. "Yes. I'll go now, but I'll be back in the morning, and it will *not* be awkward. Right?"

She gave him a raised brow look, and he laughed, but it sounded forced. He slid a hand around the back of her neck and bent his head close to hers. "Again, I'm honored. Tomorrow you're the boss, I'm the day hand, and we'll take it from there."

"Maybe my face will be a normal color by tomorrow."

He gave her a lopsided grin, then dropped a light kiss on her lips. She curled her hand around the back of his neck and pulled his lips back to hers for another few seconds before stepping back. The kiss made her feel better. More in control. He wasn't rejecting her. He was rejecting her plan.

But, what if . . .

She frowned up at him as she put more space between them. "That wasn't a mercy kiss, was it?"

The crooked grin lit her insides on fire. "Anything but. See you tomorrow, Hayley."

The lights went out in the barn as he spoke. "Déjà vu,"

she muttered. Sometimes it seemed like the power was off more than it was on.

"At least the storm seems to have passed, so the utility crews can get to work on the outage."

"Silver lining," she said as she moved to open the bay doors. Spence got into his truck and drove out of the barn, stopping to open the window.

"We're good."

It was a statement that bordered on being an order.

"Totally," she agreed, meeting his gaze dead-on. They had to be because she needed him. "See you tomorrow, Spence."

The driveway was covered in white hailstones. As Hayley made her way to the house, the kitchen lights came on in front of her, and the light over the man door of the barn came on behind her. The sodium light bulbs on the pole lamps would take longer to come on, but it appeared that the utility company wouldn't need to mobilize.

Good. She needed a hot bath, and, for that, she needed power.

Her nerves were shot—but maybe in a good way. This hadn't worked out, but she'd proven the saying that whatever doesn't kill you makes you stronger. She'd made her first attempt at finding a father for her kid. It hadn't worked out, but now she knew she could ask and survive.

Although, truth be told, there had been a few moments with Spence when she'd dearly wished that the earth would just swallow her, but it hadn't.

Now all she had to do was work with the man for the next several weeks, because he'd been correct in his assumption—she needed help on the ranch, and he was her best bet.

Chapter Seven

"YOU HAVE TO let him go," Bella said after Hayley described the previous day's humiliation.

"You mean fire him?"

"You have no other choice." Bella was not exactly known for putting herself out there, and her expression had bordered on being horrified as Hayley described asking Spence to be the father of her child and him turning her down.

"Would that I could," Hayley said. She didn't even know if she was paying him for anything other than the pipe corral, so it would be hard to fire him. "I need him. I don't know why I asked when I did. I should have waited, but—"

"You wanted an answer so that you could move forward with the procedure, tie up the legalities and all that."

Even though they were in the back corner of the Main Street Diner, and the only other patrons were sitting on the other side of the room, Hayley leaned forward and voiced her true disappointment in a whisper. "He would have been the perfect donor. He's smart and easygoing and—"

"Really, really good-looking."

They'd spent years apart since being college roomies, but

Bella could still finish Hayley's sentences for her. As if realizing where Hayley's thoughts had gone, Bella held up a hand. "Sorry. That's twice I've interrupted you."

"Don't let it happen again," Hayley said with a mock scowl. Then she sighed. "I just thought that knowing the dad personally would make things less, I don't know, chancy? I'd know for certain that the person is who they say they are."

"Would anyone else you know fit the parameters? Smart, easygoing, willing to help you have a kid, then disappear from your life."

"That sounds so . . ."

Hayley lifted her eyebrows, but Bella merely shook her head. "I am not interrupting again."

"I gave you a lead-in."

"Fine. It sounds so cold and clinical. Getting pregnant this way *is* clinical."

"And that's how I want it," Hayley said. She'd had her share of relationships, mostly short, but two had lasted well over a year, and, like her mom, she seemed to choose guys that were wrong for her. While her mom gravitated toward charming, outgoing guys—guys who were a lot like Spence—Hayley had chosen low-key guys who had their own unique foibles, as everyone did.

But foibles aside, Hayley was beginning to think that the problem might be her. Maybe she wasn't cut out to be a partner because the problems in her relationships usually started when she began to feel concerned about getting in so deep that it was going to hurt like hell when things blew up. And they would. She'd never known a relationship not to blow up. The obvious answer was to keep from getting in too deep.

"I'm going with the sperm donor catalog," Hayley said. "Those guys are carefully screened." She raised her eyebrows at Bella. "Right?"

"There have been enough AI horror stories over time to make me believe that a reputable clinic would screen carefully, thus keeping their reputation intact."

"There you go," Hayley said. "I'll just do some research."

Bella signaled the server and pulled a twenty out of her purse. "He's coming to work today?"

There was no doubt what 'he' she meant. Spence, who would not be fathering her child.

"Tomorrow. We're going to fix a fence that a tree fell on."

"You'll let me know how that goes? The working together, not the fence."

Hayley shouldered her purse before sliding out of the booth. "I will. But I can pretty much guarantee that it'll be a case of two people pretending that one never asked the other to be a baby daddy."

"WHAT'S EATING YOU?"

Spence gave Reed a questioning look before starting a new row in the wood stack, dropping a couple of half rounds of fir into place. Finally, a job that Henry wasn't doing, but only because his bursitis was flaring up.

Reed lifted two quarter rounds from the wood splitter and tossed them to the side, then placed another round on the bed. "Since you got back from Nevada, you've been preoccupied. Yesterday I assumed you were tired, but you're still miles away."

"Nothing's eating me."

"Nice try."

Spence scowled at his brother. "It's nothing."

"Was it hard coming home again?"

"No."

Reed gave a small shrug. "I thought that heading out on a job made you realize how much you miss the open road."

Spence considered for a moment. "I can't say that I heard the siren's call." It'd been a job like any other.

"You drove the speed limit?"

"Ha. Ha. Siren, like in Mrs. Bailey's mythology unit." Spence had always been more of a student than Reed, so he understood why Reed had no idea what he was talking about. He chucked more wood into the pile. "It's not the open road that draws me. I just like doing different stuff. Seeing different things."

"Which sounds like the call of the open road."

Spence let out a sigh and changed the subject. "Lex's

birthday is coming up. Any big plans?"

"She'll have a party in Bozeman with her mom and Greg and her friends, then will head down here for the weekend to celebrate with us."

"Double birthday. Nice."

"My daughter is no one's fool." Reed split another two rounds, then looked up to repeat innocently, "So what's eating you?"

Spence gave his brother a dark look. "None of your business."

"Fine."

Reed turned his attention back to the wood splitter. He probably wasn't done prying, and it occurred to Spence that his brother was a decent resource for the questions that were, yes, eating at him. Reed shared custody of his daughter with his ex-wife and her husband. It was a surprisingly friction-free relationship, with the three of them seemingly on the same page most of the time. That, he knew from the experiences of some of the divorced fathers he worked with, was something of an anomaly.

How would co-parenting work between two people who'd never been romantically involved? Like a business arrangement?

Not that he was thinking of going along with Hayley's plan. It was just that he couldn't get it out of his head, and he was kind of annoyed that this matter was on the radar at all.

No. He was annoyed that it kept . . . well . . . eating at him.

"Someone asked me to father a child."

Reed dropped the fir round he'd been carrying. It barely missed his boot before rolling a few feet.

"Someone?"

"An acquaintance."

"Ah." Reed cocked his head, waiting for the rest.

Spence hoped that his brother would assume that it was an acquaintance he'd just worked with in Nevada. It wasn't his place to out Hayley.

"It would be like a medical thing. You know . . . hand over a sample and the doctors do the rest."

Reed merely nodded. Spence didn't know if it was because he had nothing to say, or if it was because he did, but words failed him.

"I'm not wild about the idea of having a child in the world that I'm not helping to raise."

"I agree. You don't want that."

The quiet conviction in Reed's voice resonated.

"I didn't understand what parenthood would be like before Lex. I thought that it was something that you just did. I didn't understand parental instinct. I didn't realize that once you have a kid, this crazy bond occurs. It's . . . well, I can't explain it, because it's something you've got to feel. It's the reason the cows get so freaking protective of their calves."

If his wild man brother was waxing philosophic about a

bond, then Spence had no choice but to believe (a) that it existed; and (b) that it was powerful, because it had certainly changed Reed. And yes, he'd seen a sweet cow go nuts when her baby was threatened.

"Don't do it if you have no say in raising the kid. Trust me on this."

"That's what I'm thinking." He carefully set the chunk of wood he'd been holding in one hand on the stack. "I guess part of me is kind of worried about who she is going to get to father her child."

"Is this a close friend?"

Spence considered. Technically, no. But he felt a connection with Hayley that was probably based in her helping him all those years ago.

"If she wants to go it alone," Reed said when Spence didn't answer, "then I'd guess her best bet is one of those places where you read profiles and pick the characteristics you want."

"I hear some of those guys lie on the application. You know, about health history and stuff." Not that he'd studied the matter late into the night or anything.

Reed gave Spence a long look. "You're concerned about her."

"She is a friend."

"Do I know this friend?"

Spence managed to give his brother a stony-faced shake of the head. Reed was good at catching him when he pushed the truth, but he seemed to accept this silent lie.

"Did you meet up with your friend on the road?"

Which would explain the timing, but Spence could only manage so many white lies before Reed realized he wasn't getting the truth. Again, it was none of his brother's business, but Spence was used to Reed wearing him down. For his own good, his brother had said more than once, and actually, he'd been right about that a time or two.

"I guess the main thing is that I said no. I doubt she'll ask again, so it's a done deal."

"But you keep thinking about it?"

"It shocked the hell out of me," he said. Made him look at Hayley in a new way. Made it harder for him to feel like he knew all he needed to know about the woman.

It made him curious.

That, on top of the obvious attraction he had for her, would create one tangled-up situation if he allowed it to go forward. And how would his parents feel if they discovered they had a grandchild next door that they knew nothing about? There was no way he would do that to them. They doted on Lex, and Spence was well aware that his parents would love to have more grandkids.

"It is a shocker," Reed agreed.

Spence expected a joke at his expense to follow, but instead his brother set the round in the splitter and then moved the handle to start the wedge moving forward. The wood squeaked as it cleaved into two sections.

"All I can say is that I think you're doing the right thing." He set one of the halves on the bed to split again. "I wouldn't have known that before Lex. But I know it now."

"I respect your insight," Spence said. "And, moving on. When's the wedding?" The surest way he knew of to distract his brother from this unsettling subject.

"We haven't set a date. Trenna's upset about all the shit her dad's stirring up. I don't think she wants to plan a wedding until some of it gets settled."

"Do you see it getting settled?"

"Not until Hunt gets his way. According to our inside intel, Hunt wasn't all that surprised that we managed to lease water. He'd made his statement, though, and wants us to think he's going to continue chipping away until we get tired and give him right-of-way."

"Has Dad considered charging him way more than the right-of-way is worth?"

"Dad is not exactly Mr. Compromise."

"Not unless Mom has a word."

Reed smiled a little. Audrey Miller had tamed the beast before becoming Mrs. Beast. She was a partner, and also the voice of sanity, and one of the reasons that the ranch was so successful.

"Is Henry really going to retire?" Spence finished the stack and stretched his back as the splitter ripped through another round.

"He said that he'll retire at the end of June."

"He said he was retiring at the end of May too. Not that I mind. He can keep working forever, but I came home to help because, well, Henry was retiring."

"Yeah." Reed gave his brother a commiserative look. "Maybe retirement is like parenthood—you don't know what it's like until you're facing it."

Spence gave a considering nod. "You might be onto something. And, to be honest, I'm glad Henry is still working. Hayley Parker just lost another day hand, so I'm going to help her out until she hires someone."

Reed smiled a little. "Henry will be glad to hear that. Less crowded that way."

Spence tossed a twig at his brother and hit him square between the eyes.

"Is this what kind of day this is going to be?" Reed growled.

Spence put his hands up, laughing, glad that the baby daddy subject was now buried. "Nope. I'm all about peace, brother."

"Yeah. Keep it up and I'll show you peace." But Reed was smiling as he set the next round on the splitter bed.

IT WAS CRAZY, but other than her heart giving a jump when Spence pulled into the ranch, Hayley felt remarkably serene. The worst had happened—she'd asked, and he said no—but he was back to help her.

"Hey," she said when he got out of the truck.

"Hey, back." He met her gaze, and it was obvious that he wanted to get the inevitable awkwardness over and done with. "I brought you a donut."

Hayley gave him a suspicious look. A donut? The way to her heart?

Spence had no way of knowing that, but she suspected the donut was intended to smooth troubled waters.

"Did you go to Marietta?" she asked.

"Lex is visiting from Bozeman, and this is her new thing. Fried donuts. She got up early and made them for breakfast." He handed over the bag, and Hayley peeked inside. An old-fashioned buttermilk donut glistening with glaze filled the bottom of the bag.

"Big one."

Spence laughed. "Uh-huh. You can have it for lunch and dinner."

"I think I'll have it now." She pulled the donut from the bag and broke it in two, handing half to Spence, who shook his head.

"I had mine before I left."

"Have half. I'll work it off you."

There was something intimate in the way his gaze connected with hers as he took the half donut from her fingers, as if he'd finally figured some things out about her and was considering what to do with the information.

She hoped that wasn't true. She didn't want to be figured out or thought about or anything like that. But, silly her, she'd set things up to be thought about a lot with her special request.

Guess you got to live with it.

She held Spence's gaze as she bit into the donut, which had the perfect amount of crisp on the outside and moist deliciousness on the inside.

"Wow."

"I know. Lex is developing skills. While we're on the topic of my niece, would you like to come to her birthday barbecue next Sunday?"

"I . . . uh . . ."

"I understand if you don't."

"Why wouldn't I want to come?"

He gave her a look that said he knew exactly why she might not want to come. "We're good, right?"

"Yes." She pulled a sharp breath in through her nose. "Or rather, we will be, after a day working on the fence. Which leads to my next question. This is a business arrangement, right?"

He lifted an eyebrow in a way that made her wonder if he thought she was referring to getting pregnant. He wasn't, of course, because that matter was settled, which meant that she was being overly sensitive, which had to stop.

"I'm paying you to make the pipe corral. That's settled. I'm also paying you to work on the ranch. Correct?"

His eyes said no. His lips played the game. "Yes."

She gave a nod. "I have most everything we need loaded. Chainsaw, bar, handsaw, all the fencing stuff."

"Are you driving?"

"As soon as I finish the donut."

"I'll drive. You eat."

"Agreed."

Five minutes later, Hayley had opened and shut the last gate before they began traveling down a Forest Service logging road with led to the pasture where Hayley's cattle would graze during the month of July.

"I never answered you about Lex's party," Hayley said after getting back into the truck. She still had almost half a donut left, but she closed the bag by rolling down the top. Enough. She wasn't eating for two yet. "I'd like to go."

Spence didn't look at her, but the corner of his mouth turned up. "Good."

He seemed satisfied and she figured it was because they were edging back to solid ground. She'd have to make sure she didn't put them back on shaky ground until after she hired a permanent ranch hand, but she couldn't think of anything she could do that would shake things up the way the sperm donor request had, so she could probably relax in that regard.

"I'm just going to say that I'm embarrassed about yesterday." The candid statement made her feel better. Part of her initial work to overcome her shyness had been to articulate, even when it was difficult. Yesterday that strategy had done her no favors. Today she hoped it would. She would grab the proverbial bull by the horns.

"Don't be." He glanced her way, and his expression was surprisingly gentle. "From here on out, the situation is what we make it. Awkward, or congenial."

Stop that, she growled at her hormones, who began perking up at the gentle look. *You got your answer.*

Not to the question we're thinking about, her hormones whispered back.

Right.

Hayley let out a breath.

"You okay?" Spence asked.

"I was considering what you just said." The situation was what they made of it. Spence was here, on the ranch, proving that he'd moved on. She would do the same. "I agree."

Their gazes held before Spence turned his attention back to the road winding through the pines. "This road leads to a nice fishing lake. Minnow Lake. Have you ever been?"

"I'm not a fisherman, but yes, I've been to the lake. My friend Bella and I camped there once."

"I'm guessing from your tone that it didn't go well?" He had to admit to having a hard time picturing Bella Knight camping.

"It was like a cartoon," she said with a laugh. "If it could go wrong, it did. No cell service, of course, so we couldn't call anyone after the tent blew away."

Spence shot her an impressed look. "You lost your tent?"

"We didn't stake it down. We didn't think we needed to. So the tent blew away when we got out to check the horses during the storm." Now she gave him a look. "We rode in, packing our gear. Bella had never been horse camping, and I wanted to give her the full experience."

"And you did."

Hayley grinned at the memory. "Boy howdy," she said softly. "The blowing tent spooked the horses, but they didn't come untied, which was one of the only things that went right."

"You can get hypothermia on a cold, wet night."

"Which was why we headed home in the dark, leading the horses. We had rain ponchos. When we took them off after finally getting home well after midnight, they were steaming."

"You guys were in high school," he guessed.

"Yes. Junior year."

"You went horse camping, lost a tent, walked miles through a storm at night to get home."

"Yes."

He frowned her way. "And then went to school and acted like, I don't know, a couple of girls whose idea of roughing it was having to sit in a folding chair in the library instead of one of the comfy ones."

"There was more to both of us than met the eye in high school."

"I have firsthand knowledge of that. So here's what I don't get. You could take control of a situation, talk a cop out of a ticket, then drive hell-bent for election as soon as he was out of sight, but walked the halls of the school with your eyes cast down."

"Go figure," she said lightly. "Storms. Locked sheds. Snakes. Cops. None of that bothered me. A popular kid? Froze me up."

"Why?"

She considered. "I think," she said slowly, "you have to experience shyness to understand, and I don't think you will understand."

He smiled at the windshield. "No. I can't claim shyness as one of my attributes."

"That was one reason I asked you to be . . . to donate."

There. Charging at the issue head-on. If Spence was surprised, he didn't show it, but she sensed that he was.

"There's some research indicating that shyness might be genetic, and I thought I'd give my kid a fighting chance."

"Where did you inherit your shyness from?"

"Well, not my mom, obviously. I think my dad was shy. He never went out much. Seemed to like staying on the ranch, minding his own business." She smiled a little. "He was a really good dad."

"I liked him," Spence said. "I've never met your mom."

Hayley rolled her eyes. "She's . . . impressive. Looks ten years younger than she is, but it's all genetics. She's barely had any work done."

"She grew up in Marietta?"

"Barely. She left at sixteen to try modeling. She ended up back in Montana at nineteen, working at a big resort in Big Sky. She met my dad there. He was a wrangler during the summers. My grandpa was running the family ranch, and Dad was . . . let's see, how did he put it? He was discovering why he would be happy holed up on the Lone Tree for the rest of his life. And he was. After Mom, of course."

Spence pulled to a stop in front of a gate with a sign that stated, "Private Property, Stay on Road." The sign below it said, "Close Gate."

So she did.

"We're not staying on the road," she said, pointing to a barely visible track that led over a hill. "Follow that."

Spence touched his finger to his hat. "Yes, ma'am."

Chapter Eight

A S SPENCE FOLLOWED Hayley's driving instructions, he thought about her and Bella Knight dealing with a blown-away tent and a storm in the middle of the night. To the casual, self-centered high school observer, the two girls could have been neatly pigeonholed into the book-smart, no-practical-skills niche. He'd discovered that wasn't true in Hayley's case; she'd used a rock to break the hasp of the equipment shed and free him. There'd been an account in the local paper's News of Record about minor school vandalism, and he'd wondered at the time if anyone on the planet would have suspected Hayley Parker.

After the rescue, he'd started to look at her differently. The thing was, she hadn't looked back, so he'd done what he thought was the gallant thing at the time and let her be, even though he'd been intrigued by the side of Hayley that she hid so well.

Come to find out, she hadn't wanted to be left alone. Teen years sucked.

The tree that had fallen on the fence was a monster, crowned out at the top and probably four feet around. Some

of the branches were red and showing signs of beetle infesta-
tion, so it might have been the old timer's time to go. It
would have been nice, though, if it had fallen the other
direction, and if it hadn't taken another younger tree down
with it. Two trees. Messed-up fence. It was a good thing that
Hayley wasn't putting cattle in this section for a few weeks.

"We aren't getting this fixed today."

"I didn't expect to." Hayley lifted the chainsaw out of
the truck bed.

"Are you good with that?" he asked as she put on hearing
protection.

"I've had some experience."

Another Hayley-ism that would probably startle their
classmates.

"What?" she asked, and he realized he was staring.

"Just having a 'book and its cover' moment."

She laughed and, for the first time since he'd arrived at
the ranch, he felt the mood give a little. Good.

"Let's map out a plan of attack. Obviously, you'll want
the wood."

"Obviously." Hayley set the chainsaw back on the tailgate of the truck. "I've only cut logs into rounds. I've never
tackled a whole tree, you know, with limbs and everything."

"There's an art to it. I don't know it, but . . ."

She laughed again, and Spence became aware of a slow
curl of warmth moving through his body. Hayley had the
most excellent laugh. Low and husky. The kind of laugh that

left you feeling gratified if you managed to spark it. Which he'd just done. Twice.

"If it wouldn't be too much like taking over, I'll give it a shot," he said.

"Have you done this before?"

"Lots of times. We have windfalls too."

"Good. I'll watch and learn, because next time I may well be tackling it alone."

"You shouldn't use a chainsaw alone." The words came out, echoes of his dad's safety talks which Reed and Em ignored, and he and Cade listened to.

She tilted her head at him, giving him the feeling that she'd do as she damned well pleased.

More power to her. But . . . she shouldn't use a chainsaw alone. And the nutty thing was that he wanted to extract a promise from her. He wouldn't, because that would be overstepping boundaries.

But he couldn't quite let it go. "You know that, right?"

She nodded. "I had a protective father."

"Who turned you loose with a chainsaw."

"Who knew he wouldn't be around forever and wanted his daughter to know how to do everything."

Spence leaned back against the truck. "Everything?"

"There's not much on the ranch that I can't tackle. I may not be a master, but I can hold my own."

He believed her. "You hid your light well."

"Counseling helped me stop doing that." She gave him a

direct look. "Turned my life around. I could have been like my dad and holed up on the ranch because I felt uncomfortable elsewhere—like anywhere with people. Instead, I'm holed up on the ranch with some kick-ass social skills that I get to use every now and again. Like at your niece's barbecue." She cocked her head. "They know you invited me, right?"

Spence nodded, keeping his expression carefully neutral. They would know. Today. He jerked his head toward the tree. "I'll start and you can spell me."

Hayley nodded. "Sounds good, boss."

WATCHING SPENCE LAY into the old pine tree with the chainsaw was kind of awe-inspiring. He worked with the focus of a guy who knew exactly what he was doing. A guy who was used to machinery and power equipment and working with his hands. She'd been serious about learning to do everything on the ranch, but she didn't think that anyone would find it as fascinating to watch her work as she found watching Spence. She could see the muscles working beneath his blue-plaid Wrangler shirt, the thin fabric sticking to him here and there. She'd love it if he'd take his shirt off but knew that sawdust sticking to damp skin was super uncomfortable, as was hay, which was why one didn't see many shirtless cowboys, except on the cover of novels.

But it would be nice if the sightings were more common.

The saw sputtered and Spence turned it off, wiping the back of his hand over his damp forehead and leaving a smear.

"Your turn." He looked as if he didn't want to say the words, but knew that he'd better give her equal time.

"I'm only good for two tanks, then I sputter out too."

"We should be able to get it done with one." He picked up his water bottle, taking a long swig.

This would be a good time to suggest taking off his shirt.

Hayley kept her expression neutral as she turned her back to the man and filled the chainsaw tank with gas, but she was pleased that she was able to poke fun at herself. Work was eating away at any residual self-consciousness—although it appeared that she was the only one who still felt self-conscious. Spence seemed to have fully recovered from her kamikaze, baby-daddy request.

"Hey," she said after replacing the gas cap. "I might have a line on someone to take Andie's place."

"Someone who's not me?"

"You're going to be needed on your ranch at the end of the month."

"We'll see."

"What does that mean?"

"Henry promised that he'll retire then, but I'm doubtful, because he's already supposed to be retired."

"Maybe someone should talk to him and find out what's going on?"

He raised the bottle again, watching her as he drank. "We did."

"Then why . . ."

"He's afraid. That's what Reed thinks anyway, and I agree. Henry doesn't know how to fill his days."

"Send him over here." Hayley was only half kidding. She pulled down her safety glasses, adjusted her hearing protection and started the saw, following Spence's lead as she started sawing rounds from the area of the trunk where he'd taken off the branches.

And this was only the beginning. They still had to assess what they needed to fix the fence, load the rounds into the back of the truck, and make who knew how many trips to deliver the wood to the ranch. It would be great if they could get a trailer, or the two-ton truck, to the windfalls, but they'd barely gotten the pickup there. The "road" that had brought them there was a washed-out nightmare.

After the saw sputtered out, Hayley set it on the tailgate. Her muscles were vibrating from the saw and she ran a hand over her left forearm.

"Not a bad day's work," Spence said. "All we have left is the loading." He started working his way through the pieces of wood. "The T-posts are salvageable. Except this one." He touched the post that was bent to the ground with his boot, then walked uphill to the wood brace set that kept the fence from sagging too much. He took hold and shook it.

"We should replace that brace," Hayley said.

Spence nodded. He hated replacing braces, but it had to be done.

"Right." He turned to her as she pulled the band out of her hair, letting it loose around her shoulders. It looked like liquid fire, but remembering the purple hat comment, he kept his mouth shut about it.

"Let's load what we can and call it a day," Hayley said. "I need to pay the boys when I get back, and I have a bunch of stuff to do in the gardens."

"You need full-time help."

"I'm working on it," she said. "I never had labor issues before, so this is kind of new territory, but . . . yeah. Working on it. I'll have someone hired before your dad's surgery." She hoped.

The search wasn't going all that well. Social media, notices on bulletin boards, word of mouth—all that she'd gotten in the three days since she'd started looking for help were inquiries from people she knew she didn't want to hire. Either they had a rep for poor performance, or they came off as skeezy when she spoke to them on the phone. But surely there was someone hirable out there who needed work.

Spence nodded. She thought he might have had something to add, but instead, he opened the cooler, reached in and retrieved a metal water bottle, which he tossed to her. The condensation on the sides made it slippery and she almost dropped it, but didn't.

"Thanks." She unscrewed the cap as he gave her yet another of the just-a-little-too-long looks that made her wonder what was going on in his head.

"Anytime." He gave her a noncommittal half smile and, as he turned away, undid a couple of snaps on his shirt.

Hayley bit her lip, then drank.

HAYLEY AND REMY the Pig went for a walk before bed that evening. Remy still seemed to be looking for Vince, scanning the driveway as they walked, as if expecting his car to suddenly appear.

"It shouldn't be much more than a year. Two at most," Hayley promised the pig. "No matter what, you have a home with me." She might have to look into fostering another animal to keep Remy company. Adoption was also an option, but with the baby project, it seemed best not to make a long-term commitment.

The wind carried the scent of warm grass and earth, mixed with the promise of rain. Hayley hoped it was only rain and not a downpour, or hail, or any of those exciting weather events. She wanted to get the fence fixed before Spence took off again. She had a feeling that since he'd left once already, that he'd leave again as soon as he was able. It was what he did.

And you will stay here.

It was what she did. She loved her ranch, loved her life.

At times, it was a tad lonely, but she knew from watching her two parents, who lived wildly different existences, that she would choose a touch of loneliness over whirlwind romance any day. Her dad had been content with his life. Her mom—Hayley didn't know. She might get great satisfaction from starting and ending relationships.

Was that healthy?

Hayley decided not to judge. She only knew that she hated feeling things crumble around her, hated the truths she knew about a person shifting, changing.

So, if they do that, maybe they aren't truths?

"Too much serious thought," she said to the pig, who gave her a look from under her wrinkled brow. "Let's talk about you."

Her phone rang before the pig could reply, and Hayley smiled as she answered.

"Andie."

"Hey," the girl said. "I thought I'd check in and let you know that Greta is well, and everything is working out."

"Excellent." The Marvell Ranch's gain was her loss, but she was happy for Andie.

"I have ten horses to get ready for the sale in Billings in October."

"Dream job?" Hayley asked.

"The dreamiest," Andie replied with a laugh. Her tone sobered as she asked, "How are things on the Lone Tree? I heard you haven't replaced me yet."

"Spence is helping me with that monster tree, and then he's making pipe corrals."

"But he's temporary, right?"

"Afraid so. I haven't had a lot of luck finding someone full time, but come fall, there should be people available." After ranches let go their temporary summer hires.

"I'll keep my ear to the ground. If I hear anything—"

"I appreciate it."

A dust devil came bouncing down the driveway toward them, and Remy turned toward home. Hayley turned, too, hunching her shoulders against the wind.

"I asked my boss here if he thought Carter Hunt had anything to do with you not being able to replace me, and he told me that it's just the way things are sometimes."

"I agree." Hunt's beef was with the Kellers, not with her. She'd leased the water; it was a done deal. It wasn't like he could harass her into breaking the contract.

But he might want to make it unpleasant to lease water in the future.

She'd cross that bridge when she came to it. In the meantime, "Keep in touch," Hayley said as she followed Remy back to the ranch. "Stop by the Farmer's Market if you're in town. I'll give you some pansies."

"Which I would plant outside my cabin," Andie said. "But I work six days a week until the sale."

"Maybe we'll get together after the sale."

"I'd like that," Andie said, before saying goodbye.

Hayley tucked the phone into her pocket and continued toward home, several pig lengths behind Remy.

Everything had worked out for Andie and there was no reason it couldn't work out for her. Warm air wafted over her from behind as she continued down the road and, again, she could smell rain. A low rumble shook the ground beneath her feet and Remy broke into an awkward lope. Hayley also picked up the pace and, by the time she and the pig were back at the house, drops of rain were splatting on the gravel.

Remy shot into her little house, and Hayley dashed up her sidewalk. A year ago, she might have spent a rainy evening sipping tea and catching up on back episodes of her favorite television shows.

Tonight she'd drink wine and peruse the donor catalog. If she was going to have a baby next year, she had decisions to make and, being an overachiever, she wanted to be ahead of the game.

OVERWHELMING.

Hayley set her laptop aside and leaned her head back against the sofa cushion, squinting against the sun slanting in through the east-facing window. She'd made next to no progress the night before, having nodded off shortly after finishing her wine, but she made up for it by waking up early and resuming her search.

Her overwhelming search.

She was quite possibly going to have to make a spreadsheet of sperm donor characteristics, because these men were jumbling together in her head. The initial donor profiles were streamlined, listing basic physical characteristics. A quick click and Hayley could read family and medical histories, educational background and health habits. Another click and she could read an interview and listen to a personal narrative.

What if she chose wrong? What if these guys weren't who they said they were?

That's probably more of a possibility with a guy you meet the normal way.

Yes, but when you meet face-to-face, you can read vibes.

Hayley was a believer in vibes. The catalog profiles were so cold and unengaging.

She reached for the notebook where she'd been making a short list that was actually pretty long. At this rate of vetting, she might get pregnant late next year, but this wasn't a process to hurry along. Her thoughts drifted to Spence and the easy solution he'd represented.

She was glad he'd turned her down. Totally. He would have been excellent in many ways, but there was too much potential for complications.

Or maybe she was focusing on potential complications as a way to make herself feel better about being turned down.

Whatever. The result was the same. She was shopping for the father of her child in a catalog because Spence wanted to be part of his future child's life. Complications.

So why the pang of regret?

Hayley answered her question by scowling at the legal pad with the short list written on it. Because choosing a father this way was an onerous task that lent itself to overthinking.

Argh.

Hayley got up from the sofa and headed to the kitchen when she heard the tractor fire up. She and Connor and Ash had worked out a routine when they'd first hired on. They met in the afternoon to report progress and get instructions for the next day, then Hayley invited them to get a cold drink from her fridge before they headed back to Marietta to do whatever teen guys did after a long day's work. In the mornings, they simply went to work, following the instructions from the previous day.

Hayley watched through the window above the table as the tractor started moving toward the field and, a moment later, Connor whizzed by on the ATV on his way to check the waterers and mineral feeders. Any minute now, Spence's truck would pull into the ranch and park next to Ash's, and she would casually amble out the door, boots on, gloves in hand, ready to spend the day working shoulder to shoulder with the guy who made her nerves hum. She could see the two of them starting something, but she could also see it falling apart. Like her mom, she started her relationships on a high, expecting the best, only to watch things start to crack and crumble as time went on.

She turned away from the window and headed for the mudroom. It was good that Spence had turned her down. She wanted a baby, not a relationship and, even though Spence's freewheeling lifestyle indicated he wasn't a relationship guy, his insistence that he be part of his kid's life suggested that he was.

She liked the man, and with all things considered, the best place for him to be was in the friend sphere.

Which left her with the damned catalog.

"AND THAT'S IT." Spence reached out to shake the post they'd just set—the last of the eight they'd had to replace, three due to the windfall, five due to rot. The Lone Tree Ranch had long stretches of old fence, and although Spence gave the Parkers extra credit points for maintenance, all fenceposts eventually gave in to weather. Hayley had more work ahead of her in this pasture, but things were good for this year.

Hayley eased herself up onto the open tailgate, opened her water bottle and drank. Spence came to sit beside her, keeping a few inches of sun-warmed metal between them. Hayley opened the cooler next to her and pulled out his bottle, handing it to him before leaning back on her palms.

"I love ticking a project off the to-do list," she said, surveying the taut fence. "There are posts to be replaced along the boundary fence, but it's not pressing."

"What would you like to tackle next?" Spence asked.

"Pipe corrals?"

He nodded at the ground. "I can do that alone."

"Wanna bet?"

He glanced at her, caught the playful challenge in her eyes, and somehow managed to keep from leaning closer and nudging her with his shoulder. The last kiss they'd shared had convinced him that they shouldn't touch too often—or at all.

"I heard from Andie," Hayley said conversationally.

Spence accepted the shift of subjects. They'd discuss pipe corrals later. "How's she doing?"

"Well. Really well."

"Then I guess she's lucky that Carter Hunt can't take criticism."

"It did all work out in the end," Hayley agreed. "Too bad that doesn't happen all that often."

"Maybe it's a time thing."

"How so?" She shot him a curious look.

"You know . . . it may not be the end yet, so you don't know if things have worked out or not. I'm sure that Andie thought that getting fired was the end."

"And it was."

"But with time, things worked out. Like they tend to do."

"Well, aren't you the optimist?"

Spence laughed. "You make it sound like a fault."

"No. Not at all. It just smacks of . . . dare I say it?" She lifted her eyebrows in a serious way. "Romanticism?"

"What makes you think I'm not a romantic?"

"Are you?"

Her skeptical tone made him want to smile, but he kept a straight face as he said, "I have my moments." Not many, but some. He eased himself off the warm tailgate and tipped his bottle back one last time before capping it.

"Give me an example," Hayley said.

"You want specifics?" he asked as he turned toward her.

"I don't want to know about your love life," Hayley said with a wrinkle of her nose. "I want to hear about a romantic gesture or belief."

"I believe in happy endings," he said simply.

She blinked at him as if those were the last words she expected him to say. "I don't."

"For real?"

"I don't believe that *romantic* happy endings are a given," she amended. "Or common. So that makes me a . . ."

"Curmudgeon," Spence said solemnly.

Hayley burst out laughing, distracting him from the whisper of regret he'd felt at her assertion that she didn't believe in happy endings. Everyone should believe that things can work out in the end. If you don't, then . . .

He didn't know, but he went against the promise he'd made himself and moved closer to where Hayley sat on the tailgate, coming to stand directly in front of her. She met his gaze as he set a light hand on each of her knees.

"Things do work out, Hayley. Look at my parents."

"The exception that proves the rule?"

He cocked his head at her. "If you put your mind to it, you can think of other examples."

"Few and far between."

"But worth trying for, don't you think?"

She gave him a mild look that belied the steel beneath her words as she said, "I do not."

"That's sad, Hayley." He hadn't meant to say that. The words simply slipped out.

"Not for me. I like friendship, Spence. Much more manageable and comfortable and—"

"Are we friends?" Her muscles stiffened beneath his hands, then a smile curved her lips. A smile that had him wondering if she honestly felt like smiling, or if she was gaining control of the situation. Using techniques she'd learned in counseling.

"It feels like it."

Her voice was low and husky, her expression surprisingly open, considering the fact that she apparently found the topic of happy endings somewhat threatening.

"It does," he agreed, giving her knees a gentle pat before

stepping back. He felt like kissing his friend, so putting some distance between them seemed a wise move.

Hayley eased off the tailgate, dropping a few inches to the ground. "Well, old buddy, I have stuff to do to get ready for the Farmer's Market tomorrow."

"Then we should head back to the ranch, old pal."

Their gazes held for a moment, then they broke into grins at the same time, bringing relief to the moment, but not erasing the underlying tension. Spence wondered what it would take to do that. Probably a couple of miles of distance, but then he'd still be thinking about her.

Hayley shook her head and started loading tools. Spence did the same, focusing on the job at hand in an effort to keep his eyes off the woman who was starting to drive him crazy.

What was it about human nature that made you want what you couldn't have?

"NO BASIL?" CAROL Bingley, Marietta's resident gossip, gave Hayley a stern look. Hayley had no reason to feel nervous around the woman, except that she seemed to know everything, and people suspected that what she didn't know, she made up.

"The plants were just a little too small to bring this week," Hayley said. "Next week, for sure."

"Fine." Carol gave a small sniff. "I'll take these pansies."

She set down two seedling six-packs, then opened her wallet and handed Hayley her fifth twenty-dollar bill of the morning. She was going to have to find change soon if someone didn't stop by and pay with ones and fives.

She smiled at Carol after she counted out four precious one-dollar bills, then carefully set the plants in a paper bag. "Thank you."

"I'll be back for basil next week," Carol said.

"I'll set aside a couple plants for you." And she'd make sure she had a lot more change. Last week and the week before had been no problem, but this week . . .

Hayley blew out a breath as Carol turned away, then the woman abruptly turned back, effectively blocking the young couple approaching her table with a flat of tomato plants.

"You certainly have ruffled Carter Hunt's feathers," she said with a satisfied smile.

Hayley managed to stop herself from asking for details— no easy task in the face of Carol's I-know-secrets expression. This was not the time or place to delve into such matters. The young couple who'd been waiting to pay for their tomatoes moved past Carol and set the flat on the table, giving Hayley an excuse not to answer. A few seconds later, Carol drifted on to the next booth to see what kind of trouble she could stir up there, and Hayley made an effort to relax. So what if she'd stirred up Carter Hunt? He was the guy causing trouble. She was merely helping a neighbor. A friend.

Yes. She was helping a friend and his family.

And, honestly, she had ruffled the man's feathers, which felt kind of good, given his behavior.

Hayley enjoyed brisk sales for the remainder of the day, and by the time one o'clock rolled around and the vendors began breaking down their booths, she had only two bouquets of cut flowers, which she gave to the jewelry maker next to her, and a few assorted six-packs of veggie starts left.

With the exception of Carol's unsettling remark, she'd had a good day. Andie stopped by to fill her in on the new job, which was going well, and she'd gotten to chat with several old classmates and one of her former teachers. Coach Michaels, who appeared to be a fixture at the market, stopped by and purchased flowers for his wife, and Hayley wondered for the zillionth time if he was aware that she was responsible for the biggest trophy in the case at Marietta High School.

No. Of course not, but Hayley had never been one to need accolades.

She just wanted to feel good about life, good about herself. She wanted to have a baby, raise that child to the best of her ability, and pass the ranch along to the next generation. She would make a family of two, as she and her dad had been. Maybe, if she was lucky, she'd have another child and it'd be a family of three. Regardless of family size, at the end of the day, she wanted the satisfaction of knowing that she'd built a good life and that she'd done it by not taking chances that didn't need to be taken.

Other people were free to take those chances. People who didn't know the push-pull of welcoming in, then ultimately ushering out, a new stepfather every couple of years. Hayley might not have lived with her mom full time, but Reba's lifestyle had left a mark on her only daughter.

Hayley's phone rang as she turned onto the Lone Tree driveway and bumped over the cattle guard, and she felt a little flush of guilt when she saw her mom's name on the screen.

Talk about timing. She pulled over and answered.

"I . . ." Her mom cleared her throat. "I wanted to let you know that I am booking a cruise and will not be continuing the island tour with John-Paul."

John-Paul, not Jean Ralphio.

"What happened, Mom?"

"Nothing? Everything?" She sniffed. "I'm fine. In fact, I'm looking forward to getting onboard the *Seabreeze Star.*"

"Kind of a rapid change of plans."

"But necessary." Hayley was about to ask why, when Reba added, "I just wanted you to know where I am. I'll text you the cruise information."

"I appreciate it, Mom." She hesitated, then asked, "Are you okay?"

"Yes." Her mom's voice sounded stronger. "I'm looking forward to some time alone."

Hayley wondered if she needed to be concerned about

that, since she'd never known her mom to want time alone.

"Call me if . . ." Hayley cleared her throat. "Call me."

"I will. Thank you, sweetie. I'm . . . doing well." She sounded almost surprised.

"Glad to hear it, Mom. And I mean it—call me if you need to talk."

After Reba ended the call, Hayley sat for a moment. Her mom was approaching fifty. Could it be that she was now looking for something other than a guy to share her life with?

The 'looking forward to time alone' comment gave Hayley hope in that regard. She didn't want her mom to *be* alone; she just wanted her to have that capability.

SPENCE WAS PUTTING away his equipment when Hayley's truck pulled into the Lone Tree Ranch. He hadn't gotten as far as he wanted on the pipe corrals, having had to stop to help Ash with a tractor problem, but he'd made headway. He set his gloves and goggles on the tailgate of his truck, then crossed the drive to help her unload.

"Good sale day?" he asked after opening the topper door. There were empty flats and the canopy cover she used to keep the sun off, but only a few plants.

"An excellent day," she said. "If I keep this up, I'll have my greenhouse paid for in five or six years." She gave him a smiling glance, but it faded a touch too soon, leaving her with a pensive expression as she reached in to pull out the flat of plants.

"Is everything okay?"

Not a question Spence asked often, because he was a believer in people asking for opinions rather than offering unsolicited input, but there was something about her expression that caused his protective instincts to kick in.

"With me, it is." Her voice was muffled as she pulled a second flat of plants from the truck. "My mom called and gave me another reason not to believe in happy endings."

"Trouble in paradise?"

"Maybe a little."

Spence pulled the folded canopy from the truck. Together they walked to the shed where she stored the canopy and extra flats, then continued on to the greenhouse where she put the plants back to continue growing for next week. By the time they closed the greenhouse door, it was obvious that Hayley had nothing more to say.

He didn't want to press her, but if there were things—

"I'm fine," she said, as if reading his thoughts. "I think my mom might be fine too. She left what's his name—or vice versa, I don't know—and is now taking a cruise alone."

"Think she'll end it alone?"

Hayley pressed her lips together, but couldn't stop a weary smile from forming. "No," she said as she gave him a sideways look. "My mom will probably leave the ship engaged."

"Come on," Spence said with a gentle smile before jerking his head in the direction of the corrals. "I'll show you what I got done. I'm a day behind, but . . ."

"If you get anything done, it's more than I had."

"I'll finish them. It'll make sorting, loading and shipping your cows so much easier." He cocked his head at her. "How do you manage that? The sorting and loading?"

"Vince and Dad and I had a system using the old corrals, and Dad had friends who helped out at branding." She pushed her hair back. "They still help, but they're close to aging out. Connor and Ash have volunteered for this year, and Vince will come for the weekend, if I ask."

"If I'm here during fall branding, you can call on me too."

"I will," she said. "Do you think you'll be here?"

"No telling. If Dad gets back on his feet earlier than expected, as he always seems to do, or if Cade comes home for good as he's hinted, and if Henry continues to make himself useful with or without pay, there's nothing keeping me here."

"You don't want to stay?" She spoke causally, but he sensed it wasn't a casual question.

He *would* stay if he had reason, but he decided that it wasn't time for those words to cross his lips.

"Call of the open road and all that." He paraphrased what Reed had said about his traveling ways. "Speaking of which . . . Lex's party is tomorrow. Do you still plan to attend?"

"I'm not sure how 'call of the open road' brought us to a party."

"My mind jumps around a lot," he said.

She met his gaze. Smiled. The veiled concern he'd sensed when she'd asked if he wanted to stay was gone.

"What time shall I arrive?"

Chapter Nine

*Y*OU'RE GOING TO *a birthday party. No big deal. No need to feel on edge.*

But she did.

It wasn't difficult to pin down the reason. Spence. No matter how many logical pep talks she gave herself about friendship and avoiding anything beyond that, her heart jumped when she saw the man. Fine. It could jump like that all it wanted. And she could silently admire him to her heart's content. She simply had to keep it to herself.

But doing so made her feel edgy.

She wasn't a big one for secrets, and the way Spence affected her pretty much needed to stay secret. Her focus needed to be on a baby, and not complicating her life with her hot neighbor, which might affect her baby plans.

So there she was, driving into the Keller Ranch, past grazing cattle and a pivot system spraying leased water on the hayfields, with her heart beating a whole lot faster than normal. Or should she say faster than normal when she wasn't around Spence?

When was the last time she'd felt this way around someone?

It had probably been when she'd taken command of Spence's predicament and delivered him to his basketball game years ago. That had been the first time she'd really come out of her shell around someone who wasn't a close friend. It had been empowering and, looking back, it may have been impetus to the changes she began making after arriving at the university a few months later.

Yes. It most definitely had been the impetus.

Her nerves started to get the better of her as she drove under the log arch that marked the entrance to the Keller Ranch. It seemed that everyone had an arch commemorating the establishment of their ranch, except for her. Ironically, hers was one of the oldest in this part of the valley, but her family had never seen any need to proclaim the fact. The Kellers had homesteaded the area almost a decade after her great-great-great had set down roots.

Both families were considered foundation stock of their part of the valley. Reed would no doubt take over the ranch when his parents retired. She couldn't see Spence settling for long. *Call of the open road and all that.* He'd been pretty open about it.

The thought stayed with her as she rounded the last corner on the driveway and the ranch came into sight. The Keller Ranch was one of the prettiest in the valley, set against the mountains and surrounded by pastures to the timberline. She hadn't visited the place often, having no reason to, other than 4-H events that were hosted there when she was a kid.

When she got closer, she noted that there were several extra cars, and the familiar wave of self-consciousness washed over her at the prospect of meeting new people—or reacquainting herself with old—but she confidently lifted her chin and smiled as Daniel came out of the house and waved for her to park near the barn.

Fake it until you make it.

Not the counselor's exact words, but close enough. She'd been skeptical at first, which made the success of the strategy all the more amazing. People believed what they saw.

And with Spence, she saw a totally confident guy who had the world by the tail. But was that the whole story?

She parked and got out of her truck, then jumped a mile when Spence ambled out of the barn. "I didn't see you," she said, pressing a hand to her chest and smiling through the embarrassment at being so openly startled.

"I'm lucky you didn't karate chop me."

She felt herself start to relax at the teasing words and the gentle smile in his eyes. Yes, the man put her on edge, but he also had a calming effect on her. That made no sense. In fact, it was kind of confusing, and Hayley decided it was nothing she wanted to think too hard about. Better to simply go with the flow.

"I'm glad you came."

"Me too." She hoped. She sucked a breath between her teeth and looked past Spence to where Trenna Hunt and Spence's mom, Audrey, were arranging dishes on the long folding table that had been set up next to the smoker.

"We've been cooking tri tip for hours."

"I can smell it from here." She met Spence's gaze. "I should have brought a dish."

"You should relax and enjoy being a guest. Come on." He motioned toward the front yard with his head. "Let's go say hello to the birthday girl."

Their shoulders gently bumped as they headed across the driveway, and Hayley wondered if it had been an accident or if Spence sensed that, for all of her bluffing, she was still a shy girl inside, and was giving her a reassuring touch. He smiled down at her, giving her the answer. Reassurance, it was.

He seemed to be figuring her out faster than she was figuring out him.

Not that it was a contest, or that she really had any business figuring out Spence. He was a friend. One that set her hormones ablaze, but that was simply chemistry. He smiled down at her before reaching for the gate, and her stomach did a slow flip.

At that moment, she was so relieved that he'd turned down the baby request. His ability to set her off and cause her lady bits to do a happy dance would have caused complications with a capital C. With a baby involved, she wasn't allowing complications in her life. She had things mapped out from birth to graduation, and everything centered on the child—or perhaps children. There was no room for hormones and the problems they brought. Her child would not grow up the way she had until the age of eleven. She still felt the sting of feeling like she was being shoved into the background whenever a new Mr. Wonderful appeared in Reba's life.

Trenna and Audrey looked up as the gate squeaked, then Reed emerged from the house with yet another big bowl of something that smelled wonderful.

"Hey, you all know our neighbor, right?" Spence put a casual hand on Hayley's shoulder as he spoke.

Deep breath. Smile.

"Hi," she said simply. "What can I do to help?"

"How are you with icing?" Audrey asked. "Lex needs help with the cupcakes."

"Great." Hayley glanced up at Spence, who pointed to the door that Reed just came out of. Hayley went up the steps and into the cheerful kitchen, Spence close behind. A dark-haired girl who looked eerily like a feminine version of Reed in his younger days glanced up, then broke into a welcoming smile.

"Hi."

"Lex, this is Hayley Parker. Hayley, my niece, Lex."

"Nice to meet you," Hayley said as she crossed the room. "Your grandmother said that I could help you with the icing?"

"You're the person who saved the ranch," Lex said, licking the knife she held, then setting it in the sink on top of three or four other knives. "I can't help myself," she explained. "But I don't double dip, so the cupcakes are safe."

"Good to know," Hayley said, glad that she didn't have to answer the "you saved the ranch" comment. She hadn't saved the ranch, but she probably helped out.

"If you two are good, then I'll see what's shaking at the smoker," Spence said.

"We're good," Hayley said before giving Lex a warm smile.

Lex held up a cupcake with crumbs mixed with the icing. "I messed up and started when they were warm and the icing kind of sank in." She made a face as she regarded the cupcake. "Grandma had me put them in the freezer and now I'm redoing them."

"Great. Double icing," Hayley said, earning herself an approving glance.

"Indeed," Lex said with a quirky half smile. She opened a drawer and took out two knives, handing one to Hayley. "We're getting low on knives, so—"

"I get it." Hayley picked up a cupcake and then dipped the knife into the icing bowl. She'd save her knife licking until the job was done.

"Thanks for coming to my party," Lex said as she swirled icing over the top of a cupcake.

"Thanks for inviting me," Hayley said, fighting the urge to lick the icing off her fingers.

"Uncle Spence's idea. He said that you spend too much

time on your ranch."

Hayley shot the girl a quick look, then focused back on the cupcake. "I like my ranch."

"I think he wanted you here," Lex said. "Which is cool, because my dad says he's a lone wolf." She shot Hayley a look. "Spence, that it. He's the lone wolf."

Hayley managed to keep her gaze on the cupcake as she curved her lips into an obligatory smile of response. "I can see it."

She did see it.

"Middle child," Lex murmured, creating a jaunty swirl on top of the cupcake she held and smiling at the results. "Lissa, my friend who's coming for the party, is a middle. Being an only, I have lots of advantages she doesn't."

"Mmm," Hayley said noncommittally. Her thoughts had drifted in the same direction, but she hadn't expected a fifteen-year-old kid to clue in on such a thing. "You talk about it a lot?"

"All the time. Lissa says she feels like she's invisible."

Hayley gave a short laugh. "I know that feeling, but I worked at it."

"Really?" Lex gave her an uncertain look.

"Oh, yeah. And I'm an only, so sometimes it's more than birth order."

"Huh." Lex was obviously filing the information away to discuss later with her middle-child friend. "I still think it fits with Uncle Spence." Lex cocked her head in a thoughtful way. "Grandma was probably really busy with the twins. Grandpa was busy yelling at Dad to not be so much like him. Uncle Spence was on his own."

"You may be right," Hayley said, impressed by the girl's logic, which mirrored her own thoughts on the matter.

Mirrored logic aside, it was time to change the subject, because there was a good chance that anything she said might get back to Spence. She dipped her knife in the icing, then swirled it over the top of a cupcake. "It is good to get off the ranch. Thanks again for inviting me."

"The more the merrier." Lex gave Hayley a sideways look. "How do you feel about team sports?"

"COME ON, HAYLEY!" Lex bellowed from the sidelines as Hayley took her place at home plate. Apparently, a pickup softball game was a tradition with the Keller family, even though they were way short of the numbers for complete teams. There were a total of eleven people at the party: the five Kellers, Trenna Hunt, Hayley, Henry, Jay McClain—a guy who, like Andie, had once worked for Trenna's dad—and Lissa and Avery, Lex's best friends from Bozeman, who'd arrived shortly after the cupcakes were iced, much to their disappointment.

Hayley shouldered the bat. She'd never played much softball outside of PE, but she gamely took her stance.

"Wait," Spence shouted, holding up a hand to stop Audrey's pitch.

"Is this a time-out?" Daniel called.

"No. I just want a word with my player."

"Secret play?" she asked when he approached the plate.

"Just some stance adjustments," he said, his mouth close to her ear. "Spread your feet a little wider." Once she complied, he said, "Weight on the inside of your feet, balance on the balls of your feet. Relax."

"How am I supposed to relax with you so close?" she mouthed back.

"I make you nervous?"

She turned her head slightly to give him a dark glance.

"Yes. Fine. I'll back off." He did. "Eye on the ball."

"Don't give me an easy one," Hayley shouted to Audrey. She didn't want extra leeway because she'd been coached on her stance. The pitch that followed indicated that Spence's mother had taken her at her word.

"Wow," she breathed.

"Yes. Mom doesn't understand the 'slow' part of 'slow pitch.' You should see her overhand."

It took two more pitches, neither of them easy, for Hayley to smack a ball into right field.

"Run!" Spence shouted.

Hayley ran, dodged Reed on first, made it to second and stopped, then took off again when she heard Spence shouting, "Run!"

She made it past third, then reversed course and touched the makeshift base with her toe as the ball went zinging by her ear. A horn sounded, and everyone turned to see a red Ford F-250 pull to a stop. Hayley took advantage and raced for home before Henry could retrieve the ball and get it to Lissa, who was manning home.

"Cade!" Audrey dropped the ball and headed for her youngest son, who'd just gotten out of the truck and was heading for the pasture where the game was taking place. Audrey practically vaulted the fence, then enveloped her youngest son in a fierce hug. "What are you doing here?"

"I was invited?" Cade grinned down at his mom. His features were similar to Reed's and Spence's, with high cheekbones and a taut jawline, but instead of being dark, his hair was dark blond and bleached white in places.

"That was a mercy invite," Reed said as he strode toward his brother, stopping a few feet away from him.

"I knew that," Cade said with a wink at Lex. "I decided to take advantage." He shoved his thumbs in his front pockets as if trying to figure out what to do with his hands. "And I'm having some job issues."

"Quit," Audrey said at the same time Daniel said, "Find a new job."

Neither of his parents had been thrilled about Cade's latest job with a drilling company, which had him working ridiculous amounts of overtime for no extra pay as a salaried employee.

"Thinking about it. But . . . it's been a rough week. I need to decompress before I make any hard-and-fast decisions."

"You can help out here while you job hunt," Daniel said.

"I'm not at that point yet. Like I said, I might just need some R&R to put things into perspective."

"You can do better than the outfit you're working for," Audrey said with a sniff.

Cade laughed. "Maybe so. But I understand about you needing help here after the—"

Audrey cut him off by making a slashing movement over her throat. Cade laughed. "Right. The *thing*."

Spence noted that Henry, who was still standing near the picnic table, didn't seem as pleased at the development as the rest of the family, which was saying something, because Cade had always been Henry's favorite. He'd insisted that he liked all the Keller kids the same, but there was no mistaking who got to go for the most tractor and bulldozer rides. Cade had needed the extra attention because Em, his twin, seemed to suck all the oxygen out of the air wherever she went. Like Spence, Cade was somewhat overshadowed, but despite that, he and Em were practically inseparable. She was the idea woman; Cade was her second.

"So, is there food?" Cade asked.

The scent of tri tip still hung in the air, and his face fell when Reed said, "Sorry, man."

Audrey cuffed her oldest son on the shoulder. "There's

lots of food left, Cade. Sit and eat while these guys finish their grudge match."

Cade smiled. "I'll eat later. Whose team am I on?"

AFTER CADE KELLER'S unexpected arrival, the softball game became way more competitive. The youngest Keller joined his father's team, thus evening up the numbers, and the competition between the family members was on, Cade, Daniel, and Spence against Audrey, Reed, and Trenna. Lex, Jay and Lissa were on Audrey's team; Avery, Hayley, and Henry were on the patriarch's team.

The score was tied, and the trash talk had become colorful when Hayley went up to bat again. It was up to her. It was literally the bottom of the ninth, and it was her turn. No pinch hits allowed on the Keller field. If you muffed this, no one was going to hate you.

Except the members of your team.

For a friendly family game, emotions were running high.

Hayley tapped the end of the bat on home base as she simultaneously pushed aside memories of PE hell when teams were chosen, and she and Bella were nearly always the last to be picked. And that, she knew, even at the time, had more to do with social hierarchy than athletic ability, because even though she didn't put herself out there, Hayley had some ability. A girl didn't work on a ranch doing chores every morning and night without gaining a degree of fitness, but no one before Spence had ever thought to give her pointers on her batting stance. Pointers she took to heart.

Jay, who'd taken the mound from Audrey, made the mistake of sending a slow pitch that dropped over the plate—a pitch that Hayley connected with and sent flying over the fence behind Jay.

"Run!" Spence yelled.

Hayley dropped the bat and took off. She was past third before the ball came whizzing back onto the field, courtesy of Reed, who'd dashed after it. She ran for the plate, wishing that she'd done more cardio over the past year, then took a flying dive to it, eating dirt as her fingers touched the canvas bag that served as home.

A cheer went up from her team and a big hand appeared to pull her to her feet.

"We win." Spence barely let her feet touch the ground before swinging her in a circle. He laughed, then gave her a hard kiss on the lips that she was too startled to return, but inside, she melted into a gooey puddle. She put a hand on Spence's cheek, staring into his eyes as he smiled down at her, mesmerized by the intensity of his expression.

Then they were surrounded by the rest of their team, whooping and hugging and backslapping. Hayley hugged Lex and Audrey, but Jay held back after giving Spence a quick look.

Daniel ambled up, looking like a man with a back issue

who shouldn't be playing softball, and congratulated the team.

"Looks like we're doing dishes," he said to his players before jerking his head in the direction of the kitchen. "Let's get to it. The sooner we do, the sooner the marshmallows will be roasted."

Trenna gave Hayley a broad smile. She'd been a few years ahead of Hayley in school, and Hayley didn't know her well, but she liked her.

"Nice. Work." Trenna held up a fist, knuckles pointed toward Hayley, who tapped it with her own fist.

Soon everyone, the winning team and the losing, were covering dishes, shifting leftovers and cleaning the table. Cade managed to fill a plate before the food disappeared. After he finished eating, he and Reed started a fire in the old stone ring at the far end of the backyard, and Spence took advantage of the activity to pull Hayley aside.

"Nice hit," he said.

Hayley gave him a look. He was so gorgeous, and she loved the way he kissed. And she couldn't be doing that. It wasn't part of the plan. In fact, it may well upset the plan. She was looking at a biologic time crunch and she needed to act while she could. If she allowed herself to slide down this slippery slope, then it might delay matters to a point that it was too late.

But what if he was the one?

What if he isn't? Then you may well have wasted months

you don't have finding out.

Hayley felt the introversion coming on, as it still did in times of stress, and tipped up her chin. She wasn't giving in to it. Wasn't reverting.

"Thanks," she said. "I had a good coach, you know."

Spence's smile started to do things to her that she was afraid couldn't be undone if she didn't take some immediate steps. She reached up to touch his face, smiling with an edge of sadness.

His eyebrows came together, and she quickly adjusted her expression. The man could read her, and she didn't need that. What she did need was to get things back on track.

There were lines, and then there were lines. Kissing Spence was fine. Falling for him was not.

Hayley needed to get out of there before she crossed the wrong line.

HAYLEY TOOK OFF before the marshmallow-roasting fire burned down to coals, telling the group that she had a few things to get done for the next day's Farmer's Market and slipping away before Spence had a chance to talk to her.

Spence sharpened a few willow sticks for the roast and told himself to let her go, because it was actually kind of amazing that she'd come in the first place, then found Lex and wished her happy birthday.

"I'm taking off for a bit," he said. The party was over, except for the marshmallows. Her friends had headed back to Bozeman. Jay McClain had said his goodbyes and headed off to the Iron Mike's, the salvage yard where he lived and worked, and Reed had taken Trenna back to her apartment in Marietta. That left Cade, the folks, and Lex, who could roast marshmallows without him.

"Going to find Hayley?"

He gave the girl a sharp look and almost made the mistake of asking why she thought that. She gave him a sidelong glance when he didn't answer, looking so much like her dad that it was almost creepy, then said, "Sorry. None of my business." Then she said, "Lissa and Avery"—who'd left half an hour before—"think you guys make a cute couple."

"We're not a couple," he said.

"But you'd like to be."

This time he bit. "What makes you think that?"

"Uncle Spence. I have eyes. You guys spend so much time trying not to look at each other that it was kind of, I don't know, weird? And then there's that lip-lock."

"That was a victory kiss."

She gave him an *oh yeah* look. "Even without you kissing her, it's obvious that you guys like each other."

"I don't know what to say," he said honestly. Other than he hoped that Lex had some kind of secret teenage power that allowed her to notice such things, and that his mother didn't have that power.

"Go see Hayley. I won't tell."

"I hadn't planned on seeing Hayley."

"Yeah? Then what?"

"I don't know. I was just going to . . ." Go find Hayley. He would have gotten into his truck, driven for a while, then stopped at the Lone Tree. By being honest with himself, he could leave out a step and simply go see Hayley.

"Keep this to yourself?" he said to Lex. She held up her palm and he gave her a high five. "Thanks."

Now that Lex had stopped his game of oh-yeah-going-for-a-drive, he could focus on his actual motivation.

He had no idea what that was, but his gut told him to go see Hayley and he was going to do just that.

He drove straight to the Lone Tree—thank you, Lex—and parked in front of the front yard gate. The porch light came on as he strode up the walk, and Hayley opened the door, a concerned expression on her face.

"Did something happen?"

He looked down at her, then lifted his hands to her face, cradling her cheeks between his palms. "Nothing," he said before lowering his head to kiss her.

Hayley's breath caught as his lips touched hers, then she wrapped her arms around him and leaned into the kiss. When he raised his head, they were both breathless.

She studied his face, a faint frown bringing her eyebrows together and Spence eased back, suddenly feeling a touch foolish. "I actually came to talk."

"Yeah?" she stepped aside so that he could enter the house if he wanted.

He did. Spence pulled off his hat and stepped into the cheerful kitchen, setting the hat on the kitchen table.

"Why?" she asked.

"Good question," he said. He hooked a chair with the toe of his boot, pulled it out, then sat, resting one arm on the table next to his hat. "I guess I'm here for perspective."

"Okay," she said slowly.

He moistened his lips, then said, "I think I'm falling for you."

"Don't." The word fired off her lips. He blinked at her, more surprised than he should have been at her instantaneous and adamant response. She'd made things clear early on. She wanted a friend. Full stop.

That didn't stop him from asking, "Why?"

Hayley dropped her head back as if searching for an answer that would satisfy him so that he would drop the matter immediately. "Because along that path lies madness."

She said the words more to herself than to him, then leveled a look his way. "I like being your friend, Spence."

"You can't be anything else?" A friend, and whatever it was that she was afraid to be?

"Friendship works better."

"You asked me to father your child."

"With the help of a medical intervention. It's not like I invited you to my bed."

"No," he agreed. "You didn't do that."

She sucked in a breath and studied the floor, reminding him of how she used to watch the ground as she walked. Apparently, she was also reminded of that because she jerked her gaze back up again.

"I am trying to keep my life complication free so that I can have a child and give them the attention they need."

"The attention you didn't get."

"My dad was very attentive."

"You know that's not what I'm talking about."

Her gaze didn't waver as she nodded. "Yeah." She worked the edge of her shirt between her fingers, the only sign that she wasn't in complete control. She stopped the absent movement as soon as she noticed that he was watching.

"Are you tempted?" Spence asked softly.

She didn't pretend not to know what he meant. "All the time."

Her simple response made his groin feel heavy as the blood started abandoning his brain. What would it be like to feel Hayley moving beneath him?

Probably pretty damned fine.

Would he get a chance to find out?

Most assuredly not, judging by the way she was watching him. She had a boundary in that regard, and she was guarding it.

Her mouth tipped up at the corners, surprising him.

"You have no idea how often. But, Spence? Sometimes you have to sacrifice for the greater good."

"Meaning?"

"I have to look at the big picture." She made a *don't-you-see?* gesture. "You're leaving in a matter of weeks. It's what you do."

"I don't have to leave."

She gave him a look that said she wasn't buying his simplistic answer, even though it was true.

"I'd have to adjust my career," he admitted, "but that's doable." He started to step toward her, then stopped. It wasn't the time to touch. Not until they hashed this out. "I travel, but I don't have to."

"How do you know that?"

"I know."

His words seemed to alarm her.

Her mouth tightened, then she pulled out a kitchen chair and sat. Spence did the same, resting his arm on the worn oak of the kitchen table again as he angled his chair to face her.

"Here's the thing," she said. "I've had no relationship role models in my life, other than the do-opposite variety."

He nodded to show that he followed her. The more information he had, the better to make his point, which was that they should take a chance.

"I want a baby. I don't want to navigate the ins and outs of something I'm not good at while trying to raise my child.

All the instability in my life came from poor relationships. Why would I subject my kid to that?"

"You're going to go through life alone? Never having a partner?"

"My dad did after he and Mom split up."

"Do you think he was happy with that decision?"

"I think he chose what was best for him. He focused on raising me and running the ranch. It was a good life."

Which Hayley planned on echoing.

"Hayley . . ." Her name fell from his lips, but he had no words to follow with. Frustration at being the victim of a situation he had no hand in forming twisted inside of him.

Hayley lifted her chin. "I can't speak for the future, but I can speak for right now. My focus is the ranch and a baby."

Thus recreating the more stable years of her life.

She set both hands on the table in front of her. "I totally understand if you don't want to come back and finish the corrals—"

"I'm coming back." She frowned as he interrupted her. "We're even now. I said no to baby daddy. You said no to"—he gestured—"me, I guess."

"I didn't—" She let out an abrupt breath. She obviously had. "Are you sure?"

"I made a commitment." He got to his feet and picked up the hat he'd set on the table, holding it in front of him. "When I do that, Hayley, I follow through. Your corrals will be finished before I leave again."

Chapter Ten

S PENCE WAS IN a mood by the time he got back to the ranch. He would have gone to town and drunk off some of his frustrations, but he had no place to stay, no friend with a couch, so instead, he headed home.

He'd suspected going in that Hayley would have issues with him declaring his feelings, but he hadn't expected to be so flattened by her insistence that a relationship was out of the question while she raised her child. The woman meant what she said, which pretty much extinguished any glimmers of hope he had.

And the frustrating part was that he understood. She'd been happy on the ranch with her partnerless dad, while her mom demonstrated how not to have a healthy relationship time and again. Of course she equated single life with good parenting. She said she couldn't speak to the future, but when she went ahead with her baby plan, Spence was certain that pregnancy and child rearing were going to be the center of her existence.

No room for a guy who truly felt that he'd be more of an asset than a hinderance when it came to stability.

He parked the Chevy next to Reed's Dodge and sat for a moment, watching his mom move past the kitchen window, remembering the times he'd successfully snuck back into the house via his bedroom window. A good trick, that, since it had involved a tree outside his parents' bedroom window, and the branches creaked, so he had to be extra stealthy.

Well, he was past sneaking in, but he had to admit that he wouldn't mind entering his room via the tree because he didn't feel like pretending everything was normal when it wasn't.

Somewhere along the line, he'd fallen in love with stubborn Hayley Parker, who did not share his feelings, even if she admitted to being tempted to ask him to her bed. He understood her logic—but he did not agree with it. Just because she'd never experienced a healthy relationship didn't mean it wasn't possible.

A knock on the truck window scared the bejeezus out of him. He gave his brother a dark eye through the window and then opened the door. Reed stepped back and slid his thumbs into his pockets.

"Early night."

"Uh-huh."

"Things didn't go well with Hayley?"

Spence answered with another dark look.

Reed gestured toward his house with his chin. "I'll open the Whistle Pig."

Spence studied his brother. Opening the Whistle Pig was

huge. Reed guarded his good bourbon, and sharing meant that he suspected that Spence had issues.

He did. Why pretend he didn't?

Lex popped her head out of her bedroom door when Reed and Spence entered the living room, headphones on, phone in one hand. She pointed to indicate where she would be—closed up in her room—then shut the door, leaving Spence and Reed with relative privacy.

"I'm fine," Spence said after Reed handed him a glass with two fingers of bourbon.

"I know." Reed took a seat and, after standing awkwardly with his drink in one hand, Spence did the same.

"I'm not fine." He twisted his mouth sideways for a moment. "But I will be. Just waiting for the sting to end." Reed asked no questions and Spence, after studying his untouched drink, met his brother's gaze. "Did Lex say something?"

"Did she have to?" Reed asked, telling Spence that it had been obvious to everyone that he'd developed a thing for Hayley, and he hated the thought of looking like some lovesick kid in front of his family.

"Shit."

Reed smiled a little. "If it makes you feel better, when Mom brought it up over marshmallows, Cade was surprised. So maybe we've been seeing clues for a while."

"Oh yeah. Good to know." Spence dropped his head against the sofa cushion, loosely holding his glass on his thigh. "With Cade back, I'm thinking of taking off as soon as I finish Hayley's corrals." Which was only going to take a couple of days. "I'll come back for the surgery, but with Henry hanging on until the end of June, we have enough hands to handle the work here."

"One, Cade doesn't know how long he'll be here. Two, you may as well stick around for the surgery, which is in what? Less than two weeks. Three . . . doesn't Hayley need your help?"

Spence regarded his drink. "I need some time, and I don't think Hayley wants to see me for a while." But she did need his help. He'd have to think on that.

"Let's go fishing."

Spence looked up.

"Yeah. We can go to Minnow Lake. Spend a night like we used to. Fry up our catch." Reed grinned. "Maybe Cade can sneak up there and make scary sounds at night like he and Em used to do."

Spence laughed. The twins had scared the crap out of them during one such trip, to which they had not been invited. They'd gotten their revenge and then some, since Spence had broken his favorite fishing pole scrambling out of the tent.

"Sounds tempting."

"The alfalfa won't bloom for another week. Carter Hunt hasn't tried any shit. The cattle are on new pasture. We could do an overnighter while Cade is here to help the folks."

"We don't want Cade to feel left out," Spence said wryly. "He doesn't take it well."

"Let him do his best," Reed said with a grin. "What do you say?"

"Fishing doesn't solve everything." Spence smiled a little. "But it doesn't hurt either."

"Great."

"But we aren't talking about anything. Got it? We just fish and maybe discuss old times. Or your life. We can discuss that."

"We'll stay away from what you don't want to discuss."

Spence gave a solemn nod. "Deal. When do we leave?"

HAYLEY HAD REACHED for her phone half a dozen times the previous evening to call Bella and discuss what had transpired between her and Spence, but she never made the call and that worried her because, until now, she could tell Bella anything and everything.

Technically, she could still tell Bella everything. She could call her right now, but . . . she didn't want to.

Why?

She couldn't say and, more than that, she didn't want to think about it. Didn't want to analyze or characterize or theorize. She wanted to bury herself in hard work. Alone.

That wasn't going to happen because Ash and Connor would be there shortly, and Spence had been adamant about finishing the pipe corrals.

Things were fine after your baby daddy request; they'll be fine now. You're even.

But being even didn't keep her from being jumpy as hell as she waited for the man to show up. And he would. Spence was that kind of guy, so when a truck she didn't recognize appeared at the end of her driveway, Hayley was a touch mystified. Had Spence's truck broken down? It had seemed fine the night before when he drove away after turning her world upside down.

This truck was older. A sturdy-looking Ford from the mid-aughts and, as it got closer, Hayley saw that the man driving was definitely not Spence.

Had he sent a pinch hitter?

When Henry Still Smoking parked next to her truck, she had her answer. Yes. He had.

"Hi," the old man said softly after getting out of his truck. Remy nosed along behind Hayley as she left the yard and crossed to where Henry was getting out of his truck.

He was showing his age in some ways—his face was lined, and his once black hair was now more salt than pepper—but he carried himself like a much younger man. Hayley didn't know him well, but he seemed to exude honesty. What you saw was what you got, and Hayley was certain that if Henry promised something, it would be done—except when it came to retirement. Or course, that was why Spence had had the time to help her.

Was that a good thing or bad?

Well, she could say that her life was now more complicated than it had once been, and she'd spent the night assuring herself that she'd chosen the right path when she'd made it clear she was focusing on baby and ranch.

"What a fine-looking sow," Henry said as Remy sniffed at his pant leg. He scratched the pig's head, unaware that she was falling in love with him due to the attention, then said, "Spence couldn't come today, so he asked me to."

"Why couldn't he come?" A question she wished she hadn't asked.

"He's going fishing."

Hayley blinked at him. *Fishing?*

"I see." Spence had every right to go fishing, but the lack of notice, combined with his insistence that he'd finish the corrals, made the timing seem suspect. It also made her gut twist. She didn't want Spence to fall for her, but she didn't want a life without him either. How unfair was that?

"He's leaving this morning. Staying out a day or two. He said he'd finish the pipe corrals after he got back. He didn't think you were in a big hurry." Henry folded his hands over his chest and regarded her, as if trying to determine what Spence saw in her.

That was her imagination. Or guilty conscience.

"Is he going alone?"

"I guess so, because Reed is taking Lex back to Bozeman today and they said something about Spence hiking in." His face brightened. "Yes. He's probably alone. Cade didn't go, and I saw Audrey and Daniel before I left."

Everyone accounted for.

"I appreciate him sending you to take his place."

"He said there was some fencing to be done? Posts to be replaced along a boundary fence?"

"Yes. Connor and Ash should be here shortly. My alfalfa is ahead of yours. They're going to start swathing."

"Don't," Henry said before leaning down to scratch Remy's back. The pig lifted her snout and swayed with pleasure.

"Why?"

"We're going to get squalls tonight or tomorrow."

"But the weather—"

"Trust me," he said softly before standing straight and patting the side of his hip. "Rheumatism doesn't lie. I've lived with it long enough to read the signs."

"I believe you."

"A couple of days won't hurt."

Haley nodded. The hollow feeling that had started when Henry got out of his truck seemed to intensify with each passing second, even though this was how things probably needed to be.

So why was she having problems accepting it?

"I know I'm a poor second to Spence when it comes to

manhandling stuff," Henry said, "but I'm still pretty strong. I can do whatever needs done."

"I have no doubt," Hayley said.

"Fencing is kind of my thing," Henry admitted with a half smile. "If I lined up the fences I've made or repaired over the years, well, they'd probably cross the country."

"I'm glad you came," Hayley said, as she made an effort to see things without shades of emotion. The problem that had kept her up for most of the night—how to work with a guy who'd confessed developing feelings for her—had been solved, thanks to Spence's sudden yen for a fishing trip. He was either giving them the breathing room they needed, or he was upset enough at being shut down to not show up, despite saying he would.

Hailey went with the former, because she'd believed Spence when he'd said once he made a commitment, he kept it.

So why not believe that in the relationship sphere?

Because he's starting to mean way too much to you.

Her stomach knotted. She knew how these things went—everything felt possible in the starry-eyed beginning, and then reality began to set it. Good intentions went by the wayside. She'd seen it, what . . . twice herself? Five times with her mom. Seven, if she counted the two guys that Reba hadn't managed to marry before they broke up. And her dad had chosen to remain single rather than risk heartache again.

Yeah. Not going there.

She put her hand over her abdomen, then abruptly took it away when Henry followed the movement with his gaze.

Surely, he didn't know.

Of course not. Hayley worked up a smile. "I'm really glad you're here, Henry. Should we discuss pay now?"

Henry waved a hand. "Just let me help for a few days."

Hayley gave a slow nod. "All right, Henry. I will."

MINNOW LAKE WAS smaller than Spence remembered, but just as beautiful, looking very much like a blue gem set in a small granite basin. He and his siblings had spent a lot of time camping and fishing at the lake which, although situated on federal land, wasn't stocked with farmed fish and barely showed up on the map. Few people bothered to visit—but some did, so Spence surveyed the banks from where he'd stopped hiking at the top of the hill leading down to the basin. No sign of life. Just the reflection of the stands of trees that surrounded the lake on three sides, and a few ducks swimming along the periphery.

Cool.

He shifted his backpack and continued down the hill. Reed had dropped him at the end of the road leading to the lake before continuing on to Bozeman with Lex. He'd offered to drive him in, but Spence had preferred to walk, as they'd done when they were kids. Reed would join him later that afternoon with food and beer. In the meantime, Spence would set up the small tent, then fish until his brother showed. He desperately needed to calm his brainwaves after his talk with Hayley the previous evening.

A classic case of wanting what you can't have.

He wasn't certain that was one hundred percent true, but he was going with it. Somehow it stung less than admitting that he'd fallen for a woman who didn't reciprocate. Sending Henry to the Lone Tree in his place had been a stroke of genius. As he'd discussed with Reed the night before, they had a few slack days on the ranch, and Henry had jumped at the chance to make himself useful when Spence approached him with the idea.

It wasn't like he was going to avoid Hayley. He'd stop by, say goodbye, then as soon as Cade guaranteed him that he'd be the guy staying on the ranch, Spence planned to spend the remainder of the summer on the road. He'd already sent Millie a text, and he fully expected a call when he returned to the ranch, having warned her that he'd have no cellular service for a day or two.

When he arrived at the campsite where Cade and Em had terrorized him and Reed during the night, he pulled in a deep breath of alpine air, smiling at the memory. Was this where Hayley and Bella's tent had blown away?

Being the largest and nicest place to camp, he imagined it was.

And he also imagined that he was going to have to come

up with a way to keep thoughts of Hayley from bombarding his tired brain. Things weren't going to work out because she wasn't going to let them. She had a different agenda—a life on her own with a kid. A life where that kid wasn't threatened by the trauma of a broken relationship, something Hayley had firsthand experience with.

He admired her intentions, but he wished that those intentions weren't ruining him like they were.

He wasn't even going to get a shot.

"SO YOU SEE, I can't live with Thalia."

Hayley leaned on the posthole digger while Henry loosened the soil at the bottom of the shallow hole with a heavy bar, giving a small grunt every time the heavy bar struck home. This was going to take time, but they couldn't get the tractor and auger to this part of the hill, and that meant digging the holes in the rocky ground by hand.

Hayley and Henry were close to the same size and, while he was in remarkable shape, she was beginning to think that she should have handled weed control with Connor and sent muscular Ash with Henry. But she hadn't, and the plus side of the marathon hole-digging process was that she was getting to know Henry.

Henry's daughter, who lived close to Browning, had a full house—grown children, grandchildren, a few assorted nieces and nephews. She wanted Henry to move in with them, but he wasn't so sure that was a good idea.

"I mean," Henry said, as Hayley began removing loose debris from the hole with the posthole digger, "she has a big house and all, and everyone seems really happy. They all have jobs and are pulling their weight, but . . . a guy can't live like I have for forty years, then suddenly move into a . . . group." He leaned on the bar. "I like my solitude in the evenings. And the mornings. I also like to keep busy."

"No hobbies?" Hayley dumped a load of dirt on the pile next to her boots, then stabbed the diggers back into the hole.

"Why would I want a hobby? I love taking care of the ranch."

"Then why did you say you were going to retire?" Hayley stepped back to let Henry have his turn at the hole.

"I dunno." Henry stabbed the bar deep, brought it up, and stabbed again.

"Just . . . thought it was the thing to do?" she asked.

"I announced on my seventieth birthday, and yes, I thought it was the thing to do. I figured out pretty soon that it wasn't."

"Daniel will probably let you keep living on the ranch if you don't want to go to Thalia's place."

"He will," Henry agreed as he stepped away from the hole and tipped back his hat to allow air to hit his damp forehead. "But what will I do to fill my days?"

Hayley considered as she removed the last of the loose dirt from the hole, then stood back to let Henry attack with the bar again. "Maybe you could go to work here."

"I appreciate the offer, but I think they might need me on the ranch after the surgery."

Hayley met his gaze, surprised. "Reed, Spence and Cade can probably handle the workload after Daniel is out of commission."

Henry gave his head a small shake. "Reed will be there for sure. Cade, possibly. But Spence . . . he won't be there, so I should be."

Hayley's stomach tightened. "Spence is leaving? He didn't say anything." Was he doing this because she'd said it was what he did? Was he making a point, or just being Spence?

Being Spence, she decided. He'd seen the truth of what she'd said and accepted it.

"He was on the phone with his boss before he asked me to come over. I'm a shameless eavesdropper." He smiled, but Hayley read a tinge of concern in his expression. He knew that this was not welcome news. She was going to have to up her visible-reaction game.

"Oh." It was the only response she could come up with before stabbing the posthole diggers back into the hole.

"Sorry," Henry said.

She dropped the diggers into the hole and wiped her sleeve across her forehead. "Why?"

The word, meant to be casually dropped, came out on a croak. So not cool.

Henry lifted an eyebrow and gave her a look that clearly said he'd explain if she insisted.

"Never mind," she said, taking hold of the digger handles again. "The situation is complicated."

"I can tell. Spence is . . . distracted." Henry waved her away from the hole, and Hayley stepped back as he raised the bar and then hammered it down. "But he'll figure things out." He gave Hayley a quick look, then addressed the hole. "So will you."

REED DID NOT show.

At seven o'clock, Spence officially gave up on his brother, figuring that if anything serious had happened, the family would have driven to the lake, which was only five miles from the ranch, and alerted him. Therefore, whatever had kept his brother from coming was annoying, but not dire.

Spence adjusted his position, leaning back against the granite boulder next to the tent, and tipped back his beer. The air was strangely calm. Heavy, almost. He'd checked the weather before leaving that morning and other than a storm coming in later that week, the skies were supposed to be clear.

He drank again, then froze as a doe poked her head out

of the trees. After staring at him for a full minute, she edged her way to the lake. Obviously, she wasn't one of the fearless ranch deer.

Whether Reed was there or not, Spence was glad his brother had sent him fishing. Yes, his head was clearer. No, he had no ideas as to next moves other than to fall out of love with Hayley.

Was it possible to do that? To tell yourself that you're not going to care?

He could tell himself not to care, but he didn't know if he could do that. She'd gotten under his skin but good. The frustrating thing was that he knew—*knew*—that he was under hers, too, but her baby plan was more important to her than taking a chance on him.

He understood—kind of—but that didn't make it any easier to live with.

A gust of wind blew over him, seemingly coming from nowhere, rustling the edges of the tent. He'd staked that baby down, thinking about Hayley and Bella not staking theirs and not wanting to repeat their adventure. The wind passed and once again the air felt heavy. Unsettling. He didn't like the wind, but right now he wished there was more of the stuff to stir the thick air surrounding him.

He also wished he'd asked Henry for a forecast before he'd left the ranch. Henry, unlike the local weather guys, was never wrong.

HAYLEY SAT STRAIGHT up in bed when the branch hit the house, raking its way down the side and landing with a crash.

She ran downstairs, snapping on lights as she went, thankful that, for once, the power hadn't been knocked out. The wind whipped the edges of her oversized T-shirt as she stepped out onto the front porch and breathed a sigh of relief that the branch had come down the side of the house and missed her fence and Remy's little shelter.

A crack of thunder nearly lifted her off her feet and she rushed back inside, pushing the door shut against the wind. She'd hate to be out in this . . . like Spence was.

Maybe he wasn't. Maybe when the wind had started, he'd packed up and headed home like a sane person, because storms in these mountains could get intense.

Or maybe he was in a tent, riding it out.

Or maybe his tent had blown away, like hers and Bella's had.

Whatever, it wasn't her concern.

Hayley went back into the house and smoothed a hand over her hair, which had started twisting into knots during the brief time she'd been on the porch.

The thought of Spence out in the storm was killing her. She went to the window, staring at her pale reflection. The thought of him admitting that he'd fallen for her, only for her to figuratively slap him backward, also killed her a little.

She hadn't let herself think about it, had done her best to push the thoughts aside time and again, but all day, even while working with Henry, she'd felt it. Felt the sorrow and frustration and, well, anger at the man for putting forth something that threatened her well-thought-out plans.

He was falling for her.

She'd fallen for him.

Could there be a happy ever after?

What have you learned from watching your mother?

"You're not Reba." She spoke the words to herself, as if saying them aloud gave the message more credence.

You don't know that. How many successful relationships have you had?

Nothing like a small voice raining on one's parade.

But she wasn't like her mother in that regard. She wanted to live quietly on her ranch and she wanted a child, neither of which had been enough for Reba. She was like her father in those respects, happy staying in one place and being a responsible, loving parent.

But unlike her father, she didn't want to live her life alone.

Hayley started back down the hall to her bedroom, then stopped as the lights flickered. They went out, then came back on again. She stayed frozen in place for a few seconds, waiting to see what the power would decide to do, then started toward her room again, her stride purposeful. She pulled her jeans off the chair where she'd laid them a few hours before, then grabbed her hoodie off the seat and shrugged into it.

Less than a minute later, she was in her truck. As she started the engine, the pole light next to the barn went out. Sometimes she wondered why she ever bothered paying the electric bill.

She let out a sigh that stopped abruptly when another branch, much smaller than the first, but a branch all the same, came down from the old cottonwood next to the house.

This was not a night to be camping alone by a lake. This was a night very much like the one when she and Bella had lost their tent, only it hadn't rained that night. Big splats started pummeling the windshield just before a blast of lightning split the dark sky.

Hayley started the wipers and leaned over the steering wheel, squinting into the darkness that followed the lightning. All sensible deer should be nestled down for the night, but one never knew.

She turned onto the road leading to Minnow Lake, which she was almost certain Henry had said was the place where Spence was camping. Damn, but she hoped she'd heard correctly. The dirt road became slippery as the rain pounded the earth, forming rivulets that streamed over the packed dirt.

She drove slowly, jumping at each lightning bolt and the explosions of thunder, wondering if she was on a fool's mission. So what if she was? So what if she got to the lake and discovered that Spence had gone home like any sane person would have? Except for that hiking in thing. If he'd hiked in, he'd have to hike out unless his family had rescued him.

Had they? There was no cell service, so he hadn't sent an SOS, and Spence wasn't the kind to do that anyway.

He was probably sheltering in his tent, riding out the storm.

No. She didn't feel foolish checking on him. Riding to the rescue like she had in high school. Only this time, there'd be no talk of him owing her.

She shifted into a lower gear as she began descending the hill before the lake, the rain coming down so hard that the wipers couldn't keep up. As soon as she let out the clutch, she realized her mistake. The backend of her truck started sliding sideways, then the left-rear wheel caught in the deep ditch and pulled the truck sideways. Hayley fought the wheel, but the mud was too slick, and she lost the battle with water and gravity. The truck lurched to a stop broadside in the road, the rear wheels sunk in the ditch.

She revved the engine, doing her best to blast out of the predicament she was in. Mud flew, rain pounded the windshield, the truck didn't budge. Slowly, Hayley brought her forehead to rest against the steering wheel.

So much for Hayley to the rescue.

Chapter Eleven

S PENCE PROPPED HIMSELF up on his elbows after becoming aware of the light outside the tent, which was fluttering around him like something alive.

Holy shit, was there a lightning fire?

But as soon as the thought formed, he discarded it. Not in this rain. He crawled out of his sleeping bag and unzipped the tent door, poking his head out into the storm.

Holy shit again. Those were headlights. Some fool had tried to drive up to the lake during the storm.

Reed? Coming to rescue his baby brother?

Spence closed the tent door again, sat for a moment, then reached for his clothes. He was going to be soaked in no time, which brought on the danger of hypothermia, but as long as he could get out of the wind and his sleeping bag remained dry, he'd be fine.

He hoped.

Spence sucked in a breath, then opened the tent and crawled out onto the muddy ground, turning to zip it again, before standing and heading through the storm toward the headlights. The road was slippery, as granite clay roads tended to be when wet, and his feet threatened to come out from under him more than once as he approached the truck, which was broadside across the road. He barely had time to register the fact that it was Hayley's truck, not Reed's, before he took hold of the door handle, wrenched it open and climbed inside out of the rain, slamming it behind him.

Hayley sat behind the wheel, eyes wide, face pale. The overhead light began to dim into darkness now that the door was closed, but he could still see her taut expression.

"I came to rescue you," she said.

"Again?"

"Uh-huh." She nodded as if in shock, but he didn't think she was. Hayley was too levelheaded for that.

"Kind of screwed it up."

"This time."

He smiled a little, started to reach for her, then thought better of it. Even without touching her, the air between them seemed to crackle.

"We have two choices," he said. "Head back to the tent, or make ourselves comfortable here until the storm blows over."

"I think we should stay here," she said.

He nodded, then turned to look out into the blackness. The rain seemed to be abating to a degree. "Let me take a look at what we've got."

Before she could answer, he pushed the door open and jumped out onto the slippery ground, holding onto the door handle until he was certain he had his footing. He used the flashlight to do a quick check, then took advantage of a large branch and shoved it beneath the truck, getting down on his hands and knees to dig out the earth enough to wedge it tightly under the rear wheels. Then he walked around to the driver's side and opened the door, motioning Hayley to scoot over. She scooted, he got in and started the truck.

"This might not work, but . . ." He put the rig into four-low and then gently let out the clutch as he feathered the gas. The truck hesitated, then the wheels got purchase on the branch and, slowly, the vehicle lurched back onto the road.

Without a word, or even a glance at Hayley, he drove the rest of the way to the campsite.

"Wait here," he said, then got out and, in a matter of minutes, had the tent dismantled and his small amount of gear jammed into the backseat.

Then he got back in behind the wheel.

"Where to?" he asked, only half-kidding.

"My place," Hayley said. "We need to talk."

Talk. Right.

As if Spence, who was starting to shiver despite the heater being turned on high, was interested in talking. He needed to get warm. Soon.

INSTEAD OF TALKING, as soon as Hayley got Spence to her place, she started the shower, then returned to the living room and told him he was getting in.

He started to say no, but his teeth clacked together, so he simply gave her a look and headed down the hall to where the steam from the hot running water was rolling into the hall. He closed the door and Hayley went looking for something he could wear while she washed and dried his clothes. She finally came up with a robe that should cover the essentials.

She tapped on the door. "Push your clothes into the hall. I'll put them in the dryer."

A moment later, the door opened, and Spence shoved the clothes out in a wet pile, then shut the door again. Hayley scooped them up and headed for the laundry in the basement. She shoved them in the dryer, set the timer and went back upstairs, nearly jumping out of her skin when she found Spence standing in the living room, a towel wrapped around his lean waist.

"You are supposed to stay under the spray until you're warm."

"I'm warm."

"I have a robe that you can wear while your clothes dry."

"I'll stay in the towel."

"You're hard to deal with."

"Why did you drive to the campsite, Hayley? How did you even know I was there? No wait. Henry told you."

"He did."

He took a couple steps forward, then seemed to realize that she might find it awkward to converse with a half-naked man in her living room, and stopped, hitching the towel higher.

"I'll take the robe," he said softly, his gaze boring into her.

"Right." But Hayley didn't move. "I like to plan things, Spence. I like to know exactly what's going to happen and when."

"Yes. I've recognized that about you."

"And you seem happy not knowing what's happening next."

"I'm comfortable with it. I kind of like surprises in my life."

She lowered her gaze, then raised it again. "I don't know what's going to happen now."

"What do you mean?"

She pointed at the ground. "Like now. Right now. You and me. I don't know." She gave him a look that probably bordered on imploring. "You are shaking up my world."

"Sorry," he muttered.

"I don't want you to feel sorry or bad."

"What do you want, Hayley?"

She opened her mouth. Closed it. Sent a pleading look

heavenward, and then before dropping her gaze said, "I guess I want you to drop that towel."

The air went still. Or so it seemed. Hayley slowly lowered her gaze and found Spence staring at her with a skeptical expression. Then he deliberately let go of the towel, which dropped to his feet, and damn . . . he was as perfect as Hayley had always imagined. She swallowed.

What in the hell had she just done?

Something that she had no intention of undoing.

"I have condoms." She gave herself a swift mental kick after uttering the stark statement. "What I mean is that I'm not looking for, you know . . ."

"A donation?" Spence asked softly.

Hayley should have blushed, but, miracle of miracles, she did not. "Yes."

He started toward her, his erection growing with each step. Hayley didn't look away. She was too concerned with not drooling. The man was gorgeous.

"Maybe," he said, when he came to a stop only a few inches away from her, "you can tell me what you do want."

"I want you to realize that you're needed."

He frowned, drawing back a little. "Needed." He cocked his head, a faint smile forming on his gorgeous mouth as understanding dawned. "What exactly do you need, Hayley?" He reached out to undo her top button, then the one beneath it. Then the next.

Hayley shrugged out of her shirt, then undid the buttons

on her jeans and slid them down her thighs. "I need for you to keep me from thinking. I think too much."

"You do." He smiled into her eyes and ran a hand over the curve of her waist and pulled her a step closer.

"I want to stop talking," she said huskily.

"I thought that was why I was here. To talk."

"I lied," she said, meeting his gaze as she set her palms on the warm flesh of his chest.

"So this was all a trap so that you could have your way with me," he muttered, pulling her close, his skin warm and damp against her own.

"At least once before you leave again."

He stilled. "How do you know I'm . . . Henry." He let out a breath. Sensing it was not the time to talk, Hayley kept her mouth shut. Or tried. It proved to be impossible because she simply had to taste his skin, so she pressed her lips to his chest, felt his muscles tighten and his erection swell, then did it again, lightly tracing her tongue over the muscles until he tilted up her chin and claimed her mouth.

Hayley wrapped herself around him, pressing her body into his, hungry for what only he could give her. On a ten scale, she was approaching twelve by the time he scooped her up and headed down the hall to the open door that led to her bedroom. He easily carried her inside and laid her on the bed. Instead of waiting for him to do the honors, Hayley peeled out of her bra and panties before pulling him down to the sheets that were still mussed from when she'd left her bed over an hour ago to attempt a rescue, only to be rescued herself.

Spence eased onto the bed, gathering her against him, the feel of his hard body lighting her senses on fire.

It had been a while, like years, since she'd made love to a guy, but the nerves that should have made their awkward appearance did not. This felt right. Ridiculously right. Like smack-your-forehead-why-haven't-we-done-this-sooner right.

Hayley's hands roamed over Spence's body, tempting, teasing, relishing, and her lips soon followed, licking, kissing, caressing, until Spence groaned and suddenly rolled her over onto her back.

"I want this to last," he said.

"It's okay if it doesn't, because we'll have an encore."

"I'll show you an encore," Spence growled, reaching down to guide himself to her wet, slick center.

"The condom," Hayley whispered. He stopped.

"Are you—"

Hayley put her fingers on his lips, then reached with her free hand to the bedside table, where her hopeful packets of condoms were stashed. She only hoped, for Spence's sake, that they were not expired.

Spence took the condom, rolled it on. "Thank you," he said.

She answered by looping an arm around his neck and arching her body against his. Spence took the hint and slowly pushed into her, stretching her, filling her.

Making her whole.

And Hayley hadn't had a clue before this moment that she'd been anything but.

Chapter Twelve

Spence gave Hayley not one, but two encores—a personal record. Then they'd fallen asleep with arms around each other and legs tangled together. When he woke a few hours later, sunlight was streaming into the bedroom through the curtainless window.

Did life get any better than this, waking up with this woman in his arms, breathing in the sweet scent of shampoo and rain from her hair?

Yes. It would be a lot better if she reciprocated his feelings. The fact that she'd insisted on the condom told him that she'd accepted that he wouldn't father her child under the circumstances she'd laid out—although, yeah, getting pregnant on the first go wasn't likely, but still, as near as he could tell, it happened with alarming frequency.

He heard the faint sound of his phone buzzing in the kitchen, where he'd left it the night before after making certain it hadn't gotten soaked like everything else he'd had on. Fortunately, the high-tech sandwich bag he'd stored it in seemed to have done its job, because it was ringing.

Spence eased himself out of Hayley's embrace. She

stirred, then rolled over and dropped an arm over the pillow he'd just abandoned. Spence eased out of bed and strode naked into the kitchen.

"Millie."

"That job we talked about yesterday morning. It's a go."

"I'll take it."

"Let me give you the details," she said on a satisfied note.

After jotting a few particulars on the back of Hayley's grocery list, he ended the call. Okay. This was his life. He'd tried to return home. The folks and Reed seemed to love having him there, but he wasn't needed. Not with Henry and Cade both still there.

You're needed.

Right—in some ways, but not in others. He wanted to be needed in all ways.

He went to the door that Hayley had come out of the previous evening when they'd met in the living room. It led to a set of stairs that in turn led into darkness. He snapped the string on the overhead light and made his way down to the washer and dryer hugged against the far wall.

His clothes were dry, and he carried them back upstairs and down the hall to Hayley's bedroom. She pushed herself up on her elbows as he came through the door, her eyes heavy with sleep. Her welcoming smile faded as she saw that he was carrying his clothing.

"Are you leaving?"

"I have another job."

She sat up straighter, not bothering to pull the sheet over her breasts, thus messing with Spence's concentration, but he manned up and asked the question that had been niggling at him for the past several minutes.

"Last night you said that you wanted me to realize I was needed."

She gave a slow nod.

"I thought you were talking sex." He tilted his head. "Were you?"

His heart began to beat harder as he waited for her to reply. Not faster, just harder. Knock-against-his-ribs hard.

"No."

"Explain."

If Hayley was put off by the one-word demand, she didn't show it. She gathered the sheet in front of her as he sat on the edge of the bed.

"Back to my hypothesis." She pressed her mouth into a thoughtful line, as if wanting to make sure she got it right when she spoke. "You were sandwiched between a wild older brother and a rambunctious set of twins."

"Em was rambunctious. Cade was the sidekick."

"But they were twins."

"Yes, and you're right. I was not the center of attention. I think we covered this before?"

"And I'm guessing you didn't want to be the center of attention," Hayley said as if he hadn't spoken, "but you also didn't want to be squeezed out."

"What's your point, Hayley?"

"So you come home to help, and you're squeezed out again. Henry won't quit. Cade comes home. You're not needed, so you're back on the road. Doing a job a lot of people can't or won't do because of the travel. You're needed there. You do it because it fulfills a need."

Spence opened his mouth to tell her that she was wrong. Of course she was wrong.

Except . . . it made perfect sense. Hayley's theory explained why he, a guy with a stellar upbringing and family life, didn't put down roots.

He'd gone where he was needed.

"Psychobabble," he muttered, then glanced up to see that she was smiling at him.

"Want to hear some psychobabble about me?"

He did what he'd told himself he wasn't going to do and stretched out on the bed again, wondering if this was the last time his naked body would mold to hers. Hayley draped an arm over him, and he draped a leg over her. If his dick had any say in the matter, they'd soon be a lot closer than they currently were, but it wasn't time. It wouldn't be time until after he heard Hayley's side of the psychobabble.

"Sure."

"You want to take a guess first?" she asked as she traced a finger over his lower lip. He couldn't help but nip it, and she smiled.

He smiled back and stroked his hand over her hair, loving the silky feel of the deep-red strands. "Because of your mom, you're afraid of relationships." That was Hayley 101.

"And my dad never remarried, or even dated, so I figured he'd been too devastated to try and find another partner. That a single bad relationship had soured him on all. But . . . what if I'm wrong? What if he simply preferred the simplicity of being single? I know I enjoy it."

Spence's stomach knotted, but he held her gaze and nodded, indicating that she should continue.

"But while the simplicity is nice, it also gets a touch lonely. And I want a family, so I think the simplicity aspect is not a valid argument, because families do not lend themselves to simplicity."

"I can speak from experience on that one," Spence said.

Hayley pushed herself onto an elbow. "Relationships scare me, Spence. I've never seen a good one."

"I'm sorry to hear that."

"But . . . I'm smart."

He nodded.

"I can learn."

A bubble of hope started to rise inside of him. "You are good at learning."

"I overcame shyness."

"You did."

"So . . . I can learn to be a partner. To handle the ins and outs and day-to-days of being with someone without expecting things to end badly at any moment."

"I know you can."

"I could survive a bad breakup." She spoke in a determined voice. "If such a thing happened, I could be a rock for my kid if there was one. Like my dad was for me."

Spence pulled her against him, stroking her hair and her back, then smoothing a hand over the curve of her hip. "You are one of the rockiest rocks I've ever known. And if you're talking about breaking up with me . . . don't. I don't see it happening."

She laughed against his skin. "It would kill me to lose you," she said. "I don't even have you, and I'm afraid of losing you."

He went still, then lowered his chin so that he could see her face.

"First, you have me." Her lips parted, but she didn't speak, so he went on. "Second, it's stupid to not do something out of fear, right?" Spence brought a hand up to cup the back of Hayley's head. "I would do anything for you, Hayley. You say it would kill you to lose me? It would kill me to hurt you. I love you. I want to walk through life with you. But I also want to give you the chance to figure out what you want."

"You."

Spence went still, wondering if he'd heard right. Could it be that simple? "Me."

Hayley nodded. "I want you. And a family. I'm really nervous about the family part, because I don't know how much time I have."

"There's more than one way to make a family," he said in a low voice.

She smiled against his chest. "Maybe we'll explore all of them."

"I'm game for that."

"Spence . . . we haven't even dated."

He rolled onto his back, pulling her with him so that she ended up half on top of him.

"I think I've loved you since you rescued me from the equipment shed." The arm he had around her shoulders tightened.

"Right."

"I'm not kidding. I saw a girl that I didn't know existed until that day and I liked her. And now she's here with me, naked at that, and I'm not going to let her go." He met her gaze. "Not unless she wants me to."

Hayley let out a long sigh and snuggled into him. "She does not."

"Good." He closed his eyes, wondered how he was going to tell Millie that after this job, he might not be available for more. That he might have to set up shop and stay in one place, earning his living while working on the ranch—or ranches, if he counted the Lone Tree. But he had a feeling that Henry might like to work there until he was really ready to retire. If Hayley was agreeable, that was.

"Spence?"

"Hmm?"

"Can we spend the day in bed? I've never done that."

"I like that idea, but I don't know what Henry, Ash, and Connor will think when they show up for work."

"Right."

"But," he said, touching her lower lip with his index finger, "I foresee a lot more time here, and . . . especially if we're going to make a baby."

Hayley cupped his face in her hands and smiled. "There will be bumps in the road."

"No doubt. And if there are two people who can take them, it's you and me."

Epilogue

"HUNT HAS BEEN too quiet," Daniel said as he stretched his legs out.

"Maybe he's given up." Audrey glanced at the clock as she spoke. Em was due to arrive, and Audrey was obviously excited to see her only daughter.

"My dad has been too quiet," Trenna said.

"Can't you go do some top-secret spy thing and figure out what his next move is?" Lex asked.

"I don't think, given the circumstances, that my dad is going to leave me alone with his secret papers." Trenna gave Lex a gentle smile.

Spence's future sister-in-law was caught between her husband-to-be's family and her dad, but she seemed to have a firm grasp on things. She still saw her dad, but Spence knew from talking to his brother that the relationship was tenuous. Hunt hadn't expected his daughter to end up in the enemy camp, but she was his only child, so he kept the lines of communication open.

But no, he wasn't going to leave her alone with his secret papers or diary or anything like that.

"We'll take things one day at a time," Spence said.

Hayley nudged his side, and he smiled without looking at her. They, too, were taking things one day at a time as per their couples counselor's suggestion. It was early October and Spence had to say that things were going well—really well. He'd been pleasantly surprised at the first session to discover that he didn't need to drop deep, dark secrets or anything. It turned out that the counselor was a resource to help them get their relationship started right, without being sidetracked by preconceived notions and baggage from past relationships.

So, bottom line, his relationship with the woman he loved was flourishing. Henry was happily splitting his time between the Keller Ranch and the Lone Tree Ranch, and Vince had scored a small farmhouse on the outskirts of Missoula and planned to adopt Remy the Pig as soon as he moved.

Hayley still planned on becoming pregnant as soon as possible, as per her doctor's advice, but she was waiting until after their late-spring wedding ... or should he say late-spring elopement? They'd agreed that a trip to the court-house, followed by a small family party, was the perfect wedding, which worked well because Trenna and Reed were planning a huge summer blowout for their nuptials. Trenna's stepmother, Dawn, was already involved, but Spence had the feeling that no one was looping Carter Hunt into the plans. Would the man even attend his daughter's wedding?

Time would tell.

"She's here!" Audrey jumped to her feet at the sound of an engine. Lex followed her out of the room, and a moment later, the door opened. There was a rush of motion and then two huge dogs bounded into the living room, startling Daniel, who nearly fell out of his chair when one planted one front paw on either side of him.

"Daisy," Em chided from the doorway. "Feet on the floor."

The ginormous mutt grinned at Daniel, who had his hands clutched protectively under his chin, and then slowly lowered first one paw, then the other to the floor. Em leaned down to kiss her dad on the cheek.

"I'm home," she said with a grin, as she straightened up and the nearly identical white dogs—Spence guessed Great Pyrenees mixes—sat on either side of her. His sister looked like she'd slept in her clothes and her long blond hair was tied into a ponytail with a leather thong and decorated with a small feather.

Daniel lowered his hands and gave her a look. "Two-for-one sale at the pound?"

"Long story," Em said with a wave of her hand. She had a lot of those. "Where's Cade?"

"He wanted to voice his own thoughts for a while longer, so he's not showing up until tomorrow," Spence said.

Em gave her older brother a withering look. "I quit talking for Cade when he hit twenty-one. Remember?"

Actually, she'd quit when he started first grade, and Daniel and Audrey had insisted that the twins be in separate classes. The thing was that Cade was quiet, but he was no pushover. He simply let Em do her thing and quietly did his own . . . kind of like Spence had done. Huh.

Em's tone went serious. "He's really coming tomorrow?"

"He is," Audrey assured her.

Cade had returned to the job that was doing him no good because he didn't want to leave his crew high and dry, but he planned to seek employment elsewhere once the current drilling project was finished. Spence had a feeling that his brother wouldn't mind living closer to family. He always had been something of a homebody.

"Good," Em said. "I have a couple things I need to run by him." She smiled at first Trenna and then Hayley. "You guys are still hanging in there, eh?" Reed and Spence scowled at her, but she ignored them.

"It's tough, but I manage," Trenna said with a glance up at Reed. Hayley simply smiled as Spence ran a hand over her shoulder.

"I'm glad," she said, before turning to Reed. "Can you help me haul stuff in?"

The entire family got to their feet and headed out to Em's rented SUV to haul in her belongings, which amounted to four duffels and a fifty-pound bag of dog food. Spence held back and, as he suspected, the remaining family members were able to get Em's stuff in one trip, thus allowing him to take Hayley by the hand and ease her into the shadow of the big elm that he used to climb when sneaking into the house.

"I don't know if I should be alone in the dark with you," she said, once the door closed behind the last of the family as they traipsed into the house.

"That tends to lead to trouble," he said in a low voice.

"Deep trouble," she agreed, running her palms along his cheeks. He smiled down at her, barely able to see her face, but he definitely heard her as she said, "I love you, Spence."

And more than that, she needed him. Not in a fall-apart-if-he-wasn't-there way, but in a you-complete-me way. He knew because she'd told him. He'd told her the same.

He caught her hand and raised it to his lips. "Baby practice later?"

"Of course. We just have to keep at it until we get it right."

They did do well with baby practice, sometimes more than once a night if the planets aligned. "I look forward to the real deal," he said. However they chose to do it.

"Me too," Hayley whispered. "But until that happens? You, Spence Keller, are all I need."

The End

Want more? Don't miss Em and Trace's story in *Cowboy Meets Cowgirl!*

Join Tule Publishing's newsletter for more great reads and weekly deals!

If you enjoyed *Her Cowboy Baby Daddy*,
you'll love the next book in the…

Return to Keller Ranch series

Book 1: *Christmas with the Cowboy*

Book 2: *Her Cowboy Baby Daddy*

Book 3: *Cowboy Meets Cowgirl*
Coming in May 2023

Available now at your favorite online retailer!

More Books by Jeannie Watt

The Harding Brothers series

Book 1: *Catch Me, Cowboy*

Book 2: *Rescued by the Cowboy*

Book 3: *The Cowboy's Christmas*

The Holly, Idaho series

Book 1: *A Home for the Holidays*

Book 2: *Once Upon a Winter Wedding*

Book 3: *V is for Valentine*

Men of the Marvell Ranch series

Book 1: *The Cowboy's Last Rodeo*

Book 2: *A Marvell Country Christmas*

Book 3: *Challenging the Cowboy*

Book 4: *Her Cowboy Boss*

The Marvells of Montana series

Book 1: *The Montana Bride*

Book 2: *The Christmas Secret*

Book 3: *The Cowboy Rides Away*

Available now at your favorite online retailer!

About the Author

Jeannie Watt is the author of over 20 contemporary romances and the recipient of the Holt Medallion Award of Merit. She lives in a small ranching community—a place where kids really do grow up to be cowboys—with her husband, dog, cat, horses and ponies. When she's not writing, Jeannie enjoys sewing retro fashions, running, and buying lots and lots of hay.

Thank you for reading

Her Cowboy Baby Daddy

If you enjoyed this book, you can find more from all our great authors at TulePublishing.com, or from your favorite online retailer.

TULE
PUBLISHING